DEATH HAD TWO SONS

Books by Yaël Dayan

DEATH HAD TWO SONS
A NOVEL BY YAËL DAYAN

McGRAW-HILL BOOK COMPANY

New York Toronto London Sydney

To Michael, an eight year gift

DEATH HAD TWO SONS

Oh, that death had two sons so I might take one away.
—A Cretan lament

Chapter One

Yesterday he moved to a friend's flat across the road from the hospital. The old-fashioned long key turned once to let him in and he immediately registered the comforting emptiness of his new residence. The walls were recently whitewashed but everything else about the two rooms suggested a neglect and indifference which he found appealing. The floral pattern of the curtains clashed with that of the bedspread and the edges of the small carpet curled up under a small glass table covered with dust. He put his suitcase on the bed and sat next to it, carelessly drawing his name on the table's surface. The second small room had no furniture at all, and its large window opened to the street. He took off his sandals noticing the black dirt between his toes and hung his faded blue shirt on the door handle.

The suitcase was heavy with books and he moved it to the empty room, pushing the few dresses in the cupboard into the corner to make room for his one suit. There was a clean sheet under the bedspread and forgetting his dirty feet and sweaty body he lay on it.

Lying down he knew he was tired and he could feel each muscle relax separately, limbs grow heavy and the sweet sensation of the last few seconds before falling asleep.

Two large street lamps lit the entrance to the hospital and attracted summer insects. The lights were off in the large building and rows of windows were anchored to the dark hot night. An occasional ambulance emerged through the iron gate like a white sigh and with dawn the municipal sweeping-truck silently sucked in the dirt and sprayed the asphalt with water which evaporated immediately into a thin layer of mist.

There was nothing distinguished about the house Daniel moved into. A three-storeyed building, gray during the day and slightly whiter in the evening. A low stone fence separated it from the pavement and a cypress tree constituted the small front yard garden. Letter-boxes without names in the hall-way and children's writing scratched along the wall as you climbed the stairs.

He woke up. He scratched his chin, feeling the three-days growth of beard, and with what seemed like a tremendous effort propped himself up, letting his feet touch the cool tile floor, still not bothering to open his eyes.

Voices of children going to school indicated the hour and once again he reminded himself that he ought to get a new watch to replace the one Yoram was wearing when he died. He showered – not using soap simply because he did not find any in the flat – and unpacked his shaving kit. The small mirror in the bathroom was cracked, as he had expected, and he took a long time over his shave. What he saw in the mirror satisfied him. A mature face reflecting his thirty years accurately, sharp features, dark blond hair and gray eyes. He carefully removed a pimple from the side of his straight nose and enjoyed the otherwise smooth and healthy look of his pale skin. He was too tall for Rina's mirror, almost too tall for her bed, but he was not going to stay there long, not a day longer than necessary, and with this thought he walked through the empty room to open the window.

The children were gone and the street had assumed its mid-morning routine. In the café down below a few nurses were giggling – odd to see nurses in uniform away from the hospital corridors and realize how unaffected they were by the proximity of heavy breathing – and a steady stream of people went in and out of the door marked ' Out-Patients '. Two old beggars were sitting in front of the high wall surrounding the hospital, offering prayers for the sick for as little as a few piastres. Through the second floor windows, he could see a group of doctors making their morning rounds with the severe importance of divine judges.

Daniel pulled a chair to the window, arranged the books on the window-sill and prepared himself for a long watch.

As from tomorrow, this white group of men would stop in front of a bed in one of the rooms. They would pick up the temperature-chart tied to the iron bar and give the old man a professional encouraging smile. The name on the board would be Haim Kalinsky and he would be spending his last few days in the municipal hospital where he would die of cancer of the lungs.

Haim Kalinsky, his file would disclose, was born sixty-five years ago in Warsaw and had been a citizen of Israel and a resident in Beer-Sheba since 1960. A few lines in Latin would define the malignant tumour, advanced stage, first suspected two weeks earlier. At the bottom of the page the column headed ' Immediate Relations ' would indicate that Kalinsky had one son, living in Tel-Aviv, and that his second wife and daughter could be reached by telephone in case of an emergency.

11

It was noon. The cypress tree looked weird, shadowless and the dry desert air hovered still between the morning dust and the afternoon breeze. A few days earlier Daniel had received the letter from Miriam Kalinsky. It was brief – what was there to say? – and informed him of the date her father would be entering the hospital. There was no need to refer to his grave condition. Although she did not think he would, she suggested he should visit the dying man. Following the letter, a conversation with Rina, who was excavating in the south and kept the flat in Beer-Sheba for week-ends, then a long and slow bus trip to the desert city which he knew so well, and now the window and the hospital across the road and the feeling that they would not bring his father in before dusk.

Those of the sick who could walk, stood framed in windows watching the street below. They had in common a jealous stare at everything that was healthy and fast and free, and the gentle expression of resignation to their light blue hospital robes, and their catalogued, filed and re-searched diseases. When Daniel felt he was being stared at he was embarrassed and covered his large torso with an old army shirt. Food was being served in the second-floor ward and he could imagine the lack of appetite with which it was being consumed. Smiling nurses now pulled the curtains one by one to allow the patients their afternoon sleep, depriving him of the view. The sun was above the old mosque sending cruel arrows toward the hospital windows and Daniel walked down to the café.

The ' Café Tikva ' was run by a Rumanian couple. Mr Lipsky – or just ' Lipsky ' to the customers – was short and thin and his white apron hung loose on his body. His wife had a small round head set on an enormous body which in turn was balanced on short and rather pretty legs. Her

12

hair was curly and the yellow tint that helped its colour was not applied to her upper lip which boasted a thin but quite dark moustache. Two large fans seemed to produce only whirlpools of dust on the cement floor and the terrace, which opened to the street, was lit at night with two rows of painted blue, yellow and red bulbs.

Daniel walked in and ordered coffee and newspapers. Lipsky recommended the pickled herring and as he got no answer he brought it along anyway with fresh brown bread and onion rings.

Two doctors were reading evening papers in the corner and the sound of the fan was disturbed by an occasional sigh from Mrs Lipsky which held complaint of the sun, the dust, the heat, the Bedouins – everything that was not Bucharest.

At quarter-past six he saw them coming, Miriam's husband and Miriam and her father. She helped her father out of the taxi while her husband paid the driver and carried the small suitcase. By mistake they walked to the door marked ' Out-Patients ' and then returned to the main entrance. Mr Kalinsky was wearing a suit, as if going to a funeral or a wedding – nobody else wears suits in Beer-Sheba in the summer – and Miriam had a scarf over her long dark hair. Her husband kept wiping his neck with a handkerchief and Daniel could not see their faces. Were they worried? relieved? hopeful? They disappeared just as the doors were opened to visitors carrying flowers, boxes of chocolate, or packages of fruit, and he imagined them going through the large reception hall which he knew well. They were filling in the forms now, he thought, and her father would be given a robe, light blue pyjamas and a small towel. They would take away his personal belongings to be returned when he left the hospital, and Daniel wondered what it was that he carried in the suitcase. A book in Polish probably, the Bible, reading glasses, perhaps some photographs.

They are climbing the stairs now, he thought, and the old man is being taken by the nurse to change. Miriam would look at the watch – is it time to feed the child ? – and her father would return dressed in blue feeling awkward and shy in the starched wide pyjamas.

He was allotted a bed on the second floor; Daniel could see Miriam opening the window – the second from the left corner – arranging some things in the small bed-side cupboard. A few minutes later the couple left the hospital, looked up towards the window – where nobody was standing – and began to walk up towards the main road. It was then that Daniel waved and caught Miriam's eye.

She whispered something to her husband who nodded and waved and waved again to Daniel and walked hurriedly away. She climbed the few stairs, saying hello to Lipsky who was smoking on the terrace and entered the café.

*　　*　　*

They shook hands and Miriam ordered some tea. She was an attractive woman, though not beautiful. Her small nose and mouth gave her face a childish air which the mature experienced eyes belied. She removed her scarf to let her long black hair down her shoulders and with small rough hands fumbled in her straw purse for some cigarettes.

' I did not think you'd come,' she said. She had a way of staring at him which made him lower his eyes.

' How is he? '

' We don't know yet. When I wrote you it was after the

14

first test. It's definite but they don't know how long he's got.'

' Pain? '

' No. Headaches, weakness – nothing to make him suspect he was not well, or to make him see a doctor sooner.'

' He's lost a lot of weight.'

' Yes, that was why we insisted he should have a check-up. He was coughing and it wouldn't stop. We should know more by the end of the week. You'll stay won't you? '

' How much does he know now? '

' All or nothing,' she muttered. ' Who knows? He's not dramatic about it. We took him today and he behaved like a child. Shy and resigned. He knows what's wrong, he doesn't talk about it. He's seen the results of the test and he only nodded when we suggested it could be operated and removed.'

' Do you think he is a brave man? ' This he asked himself really but again her look penetrated him and there was sweat on his palms.

' Either too much of a coward to face it – or the bravest, facing it in solitude, not sharing the fear. Perhaps we'll never find out. I have to go home now.'

He waited for her to ask him something. Couldn't she simply face him with it? Say, ' will you visit him? '

She asked him whether she could leave the child with him on Saturday because she wanted to come for the whole day.

' Of course. I live here, across the road. A friend's flat, third floor.'

' Very convenient.' She tied her scarf around her hair which made her look younger.

' Where is your mother, isn't she coming? '

' She's not well. Nothing serious ' – she smiled now for the first time – ' but she has to stay in bed for a few days. We didn't tell her about the test, so she thinks he's in for a check-up – anaemia and so on.' She got up to go.

' Your cigarettes.' He gave her the packet and she smiled warmly again.

' He asked about you today. Shall I tell him you're here? '

' You don't have to.'

She said shalom to Lipsky and left. Daniel watched her small figure hurry up the street. The windows of the hospital were all lit now.

Daniel went back to the flat, showered again, dressed and walked out. He felt hungry, for the first time since he arrived, and strolled towards the centre of town. No air is more engulfing than desert evening air. Its dryness seems to brush the skin with rough warm hands and rest there a while before giving way to a new wave of caressing breeze. The moon was not up yet but the white sand seemed to reflect the last rays of sun until it enjoyed the incestuous encounter with the moon, for surely the surface of the moon must resemble those endless cracked white plains surrounding the city.

The town of Abraham looks like an incomplete cross-word puzzle. Clusters of buildings and between them desert patches awaiting their turn to be built upon. Roads which end suddenly on a verge of a wadi bed and asphalt tracks disappearing under dune sand to reappear later, shining black against the white. The eucalyptus trees planted along the streets were fifteen years old but pale and underdeveloped. They looked pathetic, clinging to life, searching for water in vain in the depth of this salty

16

womb.

Daniel approached the centre of the city which offered no skyline, no silhouettes. The houses merged with the scenery and only the minaret and a few palm trees jerked up, monuments to old times when the city was an oasis in the caravan path.

The popular restaurant in town was called ' Morris's ' and he had no difficulty in finding it in one of the side streets branching from the main road leading south.

As if ten years had not gone by.

Was he really ten years older than the soldiers who crowded the restaurant? The laughing girl-soldiers with white headwear around their necks haven't changed, and the dusty jeeps parked in front could be his unit's. The menu was the same. Would he be surprised if Yoram and Rina were to enter through the glass door?

Heavy boots on soldiers' feet rested slumped under the tables. Did they still say to each other when down south on patrol, ' see you at Morris's '? Did they too, when driving north and reaching the plateau, associate the city's lights with cold beer and kebab?

The waitress had a comfortable lazy look about her and a strong French accent.

' Beer and kebab,' he said, uttering his thoughts rather than ordering.

' Salad? '

' Yes, salad. With onions.'

He had no gray hair and his skin was smooth all over. He could still swim across the lake and climb any mountain. He felt a gentle tremble touching the hair of a girl for the first time and still enjoyed Winnie the Pooh, so where did the ten years go? The smell of tanks' oil and rubber tracks was fresh in his nostrils and the memory of the

17

silence before an ambush still tensed his nerve-ends. The cold beer had the same bitterness on his palate and he could recite the Song of Songs. Could it be only the dates in the calendar that change, and other people? Was it supposed to happen suddenly with the shock of wrinkles and baldness and flabby flesh? The waitress brought the salad and some coffee and fruit.

Back in the main street he walked toward the police station and turned left into a dusty road. A few cars were parked in front of the bar's entrance and a large wrought-iron sign read ' The Last Chance '.

On high stools around the bar sat three men. Two officers and three girls were sprawled on mattresses which had been turned into sofas against the wall and two mangy dogs slept under an old clock which had stopped some time ago – its hands at quarter-past six. He joined the men and ordered a beer.

The man next to him was addressed as ' Doctor' by the bar owner, and Daniel turned to him.

' Are you a physician? '

' Yes. Municipal hospital. Still in the army though.'

Daniel introduced himself.

' Can I ask you a question – a professional one? '

' Of course. Are you sick or something? Everybody remembers their diseases when they meet a doctor.'

' No. A friend is. Could you tell me about lung-cancer? '

' Not my ward. I'm an orthopaedic surgeon. Still, what would you like to know? It's quite common, that is as cancers go. What happens is that the cells of the membrane lining in the air passages in a lung, or both lungs, undergo a change. This leads to uncontrolled cell growths – what you call a malignant tumour. The tumour invades and destroys the contiguous structure and finally blocks the

18

air passages. It can also spread through the lymph channels and the blood stream, to other parts of the body, unless you operate on it early enough.'

' And if not? '

The doctor looked serious now, because the earlier description was given with the condescension accompanying a professional reading of fact to a layman.

' If not, the usual. Second-floor ward, treatment, cobalt radiation, drugs, morphine for pain and the long wait.'

' How long?'

' It depends on the phase. Can't really tell you. A haemorrhage speeds the process sometimes. I wish I could tell you more. How old is he? '

' In his sixties. Thank you.'

' Don't mention it. I am sorry about it. Do you live here? '

' No, just visiting.'

Small talk, another beer, hand-shake and the row of street lamps swaying lightly. The moon now was pierced in the sky by the minaret and when it finally liberated itself it was trapped by the palm branches. The pebbles in Wadi Beer-Sheba glistened and Daniel took the path across the bridge into the wadi. How misleading, he thought. In the winter the wadi turned into a dangerous river, sweeping away the unsuspecting in its path. And come summer, it was this dry innocence, tragic like a childless woman, pitiful like a useless belt bordering the southern suburbs of the city.

Well, Kalinsky, he thought, it's a long way from the Vistula to the wadi, from Poniatowski Bridge in Warsaw to the Beer-Sheba Bridge. You were born near the one, and you are dying right now so near the other. Not really dying, as this demands participation, awareness – death is happening to you. How did the doctor put it Kalinsky? The malignant tumour, in its inevitable majesty, invades and destroys the contiguous structures and blocks the air passages. Does it feel like worms eating you up or like a warm liquid spreading slowly, or is it an heroic enemy thrusting in and pushing its way to corners, to air passages, to tissues, sometimes to the lymph-channel he said – has it reached the lymph-channels yet?

Do you lie there covered with a thin over-washed over-sterilized sheet thinking you have bad bronchitis or do you sense it is bronchogenic carcinoma and talk to it, frighten it away, match its guts, gather all your strength and splendour – the way they say some people do – and combat it clinging to every bit of tissue which is not yet diseased?

They say men display unexpected courage in their fight to survive. You are not a brave man Kalinsky, do you display this courage? You know you are dying. You must know, you have seen the tests. The black X-ray sheet with the white bones symmetrical, healthy and the visiting tumour you nursed and fed and sheltered.

The driftwood looks like dried bones in the wadi-bed. Was that what Ezekiel saw, a valley full of driftwood? Daniel sat on a large stone and enjoyed the cold feel of pebbles. They were smooth to touch and dry, as it is only at dawn that the dew blesses the dust, the stones and the thirsty leaves.

It's the end of a long way Kalinsky, considering the number of times you were close to the coffin. I sound harsh, almost as if I wished you dead – how could I? But the doctor said – the usual. Not a special spectacular disease and death, not one with a long exotic name, not even a variation on a cancer like Hodgkin's or leukaemia,

20

just plain lung-cancer, another figure for the statisticians. To think how many death traps you've escaped, trusting in God and paying the price and committing yourself to faith which proved a worthy companion, and now – it is quite common, he said. It would have been proper for common people to die of uncommon diseases to crown their common life. Names which never appeared in print could be perpetuated by autopsy reports in professional research books.

Were you a common man Kalinsky? The tumour does not choose. It is everywhere and perhaps right now in the little mole on my left arm. Or perhaps in the bone of my big toe playing with the pebble an agent is slowly working its way into the bloodstream. Do we breathe it? Or consume it with food? Is it God-sent, the way the ancients believed their more human enemies were?

You are a common man, but you had an uncommon moment once, and this makes you very distinguished and special.

We never talked about it, and it hung between us since we met, and we shall never talk about it and though it has remained alive and scarring all these years it will die with you.

Back in Poland, for the millionth time Daniel reconstructed the story as if he were doomed to night after night. You must remember your house, the first one? In the Muranow quarter. The large piano and the blue-glass vase on it, always with fresh flowers. Family portraits and two oil-paintings of your two sons. It does not matter that with so many others you shuddered on the 1st of October when Hitler entered Warsaw and when you left the house for the Ghetto you buried the gold in the back-yard and burnt the business papers and put on your best suit as did

21

your wife.

Do you remember how she was taken away when you were out, and you cried and hugged your sons and said she will be back?

You were still a common man then. A merchant, an honest one I believe, caring for the family and attending services on Yom Kippur. You were never faced with extraordinary situations and your anger or joy or distress had the easy certainty of the middle of the road. Not too much, not too excited, not to get too angry, everything will be all right. You did cry when she was gone and perhaps for once you did not take her for granted and for a few days, until they came for you and your sons, you loved her like you never loved before – the love that depends and misses and longs. The love sent from you, lying there, towards the other bed met an irreplaceable emptiness and crawled back to you chokingly. You always had separate beds, didn't you ? Still, this is not what made you special, because thousands were lying in dark rooms with an emptiness at their side and frustrated anger that could just reach the fists, no farther.

Then they came for you and the boys. Do you remember, Haim Kalinsky, how good-looking they were ? One dark and wiry with brown dreamy eyes – resembling you, kind and friendly and very talented, they said. He was eleven then. He played the piano. He had a golden voice and long fingers and you loved him so much. And the younger, with his mother's blond hair and gray eyes and long limbs? He was his mother's favourite, and he believed you when you said she would be back.

You did not cry when they came for you. You took the boys by the hand and when your little boy asked how would his mother know where he was , you said she would, and told him not to cry.

Then came that winter day. You were taken out of the line with both boys to a yard behind the barracks.

You held your big boy's hand and he held his brother's and you were still wearing your best clothes as if going for a walk in Lazienki Park. The officers were armed and they told you to stop. You all spoke Yiddish at home so you could understand their German when they told you how nice your boys were. You smiled back – a horrified smile it was – and patted Shmuel's head, he was nearer to you.

They are so nice, they said, you can have the choice.

Did you really not understand what they meant? You told them you did not. There wasn't much time, they said. You could choose the one who would be shot and be left with the other.

You did not believe it. How could you? Yet it was a human brain that invented such a simple torture and you were given your moment. What went through your heart then? Did anything? You turned away from the boys and covered your face and screamed. They said they would take both unless you decided and when you turned to look at them – it was a question of seconds – you were never to be the same man again. You were trembling and you were Abraham, and you were God. You could give or take away a life and you grabbed Shmuel who was weeping and could not bear to look at his blond slim brother who made no attempt to hold you or speak, or understand, and you turned your back.

Why didn't you kiss me then father?

Did you think they would kill me there and then? Is that why you hurried so?

They led me away laughing and talking, they gave me a bar of chocolate.

23

Chapter Two

The small boat was sailing from Bari under a Greek flag. The war was just over and the late summer winds hurried it on its course. A special section was allotted to parentless children and a young volunteer was responsible for them. Daniel Kalinsky was a shy boy and hardly talked even with the other Polish children. He did not know how old he was, so judging by his mature eyes rather than by his undernourished body they put down eleven, with a question mark in brackets. Another question mark next to the parents' names. They were both marked dead, with a question mark, but this was routine – they were bound to be dead. He could not, or would not, give an accurate description of his parents. She was beautiful was all he had to say about his mother, and as for Haim Kalinsky he could not be made to talk about him. All that was left with him was the memory of the last moments he saw his father, and this memory he could not share. If only by childish intuition, somehow he knew that it was horribly wrong to mention it, not even to Yoram who was always there pulling faces trying to make him laugh, giving him chocolates, or singing Hebrew songs to him which he did not understand. His head was shaved and he was given clothes – too large for him but clean and dry.

Most of the short journey Daniel suffered from sea-sickness and during the illegal landing he was simply carried by Yoram, like a bundle, to the front seat of a truck where he dozed off. He woke up in the wooden house which served as a dining room in Kibbutz Gilad.

He let himself be led by the hand with three other children once he assured himself that Yoram was there – though walking in another direction. The Kibbutz secretariat, after a long discussion, agreed that it would be best not to isolate the adopted children but scatter them among their own. So Daniel was installed with one boy who arrived with him and two other boys his age who were born on the farm.

During the following few days he was initiated in the way of life of Gilad and he seemed to accept it neither happily nor sadly. He was definitely a well-educated boy and during meals when he was offered food he thanked the girl who served him, in Polish, without a smile. He understood he was in Israel, made no effort to speak the few Hebrew words he had learned on the boat and followed the others in a quiet disciplined way which evoked kind looks from the housekeeper suggesting that she understood how long it took for a grown-up to retrieve his childishness.

His hair was growing now, which gave him an itchy sensation, and the new clothes he was given fitted him although for a while he refused to wear sandals without socks or unbutton the collar of his shirt. A woman called Rivka was responsible for the children during their off-school hours and Joseph was their teacher. They both could speak Yiddish and although conversation with Daniel was limited, he answered whenever addressed. Yoram had to leave for Europe to escort another party of refugees and he came to say goodbye to Daniel. Be good, he told him, and laid his hand on the boy's shoulder which sent a shiver through his little body. Rivka was in the room to translate the – when will you be back? – and Yoram laughed heartily. In two weeks he said. He left, and Daniel followed him to the truck unnoticed. When Yoram got into the car Daniel was behind a house waving without being seen and exactly two weeks later Rivka found the boy on the main road leading to Gilad sitting on a mile-stone. He told her he was waiting for Yoram, though he never mentioned him when he was gone, and she explained that the boat was due any night but it might be impossible to land which would cause a delay.

The 'adopted children' were given Hebrew lessons separately, the first words not being the usual '*Shalom Aba, Shalom Ima*' ('hello mother', 'hello father') but rather '*Chaver*', '*Chavera*' and '*Moreh*' ('comrade', 'teacher'). Daniel was a good pupil although he was not as anxious to use the new words as other children were. He wrote with great ease and the teacher encouraged his reading by giving him more advanced books. In three months they would be ready to join their age-groups in school, with whom they now shared the after-school hours of work on the farm.

Yoram came back with more children and Daniel watched them – older children this time – descend from the truck and be taken to rooms. Yoram came to see him in the evening, just when the parents of the two Gilad boys were putting them to bed – they were very good about it and never forgot to say a warm goodnight and tuck in the two boys who were not their own – and this time Daniel did not try to hide his excitement. He could form a few sentences and when Yoram tucked him in and turned to go, he held onto his hand and made him sit on the edge of the bed until his eyes felt heavy and he fell asleep.

Several small crises marked his period of adjustment in an obvious way – like an unwilled exclamation of fear first time in the cowshed when a cow seemed to charge towards him. The other children laughed and he withdrew into himself for the rest of the day while Rivka explained to them the background of the ' adopted children '.

There was a piano in the culture-room and the children were taken there one afternoon to listen to a recital – light and easy compositions – given by a guest from town. With the first notes which filled the room Daniel burst into tears and – as with several similar outbursts – they had to call on Yoram to comfort him. He did not tell Yoram about Shmuel but finally relaxed and was excused from all music lessons.

A minor crisis occurred when one of the boys celebrated his birthday. He was given a few gifts and Yoram played the accordion for the children who were sitting on the lawn in front of their house. A large cake was distributed and the boy was placed on a chair and lifted twelve times – and one for next year. When Daniel asked when his birthday would be celebrated and the answer was slow to come, he left the room about to cry. Rivka and Joseph discussed the problem, which applied to other children as well, and during dinner Daniel received a piece of paper with a date on it. Even when he found out his real birth date many years later, he still celebrated it according to Rivka's note.

When Joseph and Rivka had to write a report about Daniel Kalinsky it was a very short one. ' Developing satisfactorily considering past hazards. Industrious pupil with an unusual ability and tendency to express himself in

27

writing. Overcame shyness with great difficulties but now participates in social activities. Seems to enjoy physical farm work. Sleeps well and never complains of disturbing dreams. Refuses to refer to the past but it seems that he remembers very little – if any – of his home life in Warsaw. Very attached to Yoram and displays towards him jealousy, moodiness and tenderness which are not as evident in his relations with school mates. Perfect health.'

No nightmares, no visions of parents invading the smoke of kerosene stove in winter and no ghosts emerging from morning mists in the summer. Yoram was there, only six years his senior, training underground recruits now and on Saturdays they went for long walks along the fields' tracks. He learned from Yoram the names of flowers, the names of birds, the names of the mountains across the Jordan River and the tunes of songs. Yoram was short and round-faced, blessed with laughter in the pupils of his eyes and hands too large for his body. He had brown curls – trimmed too seldom – and if not handsome, there was a charitable quality to his features which lent his face the beauty that comes from innocent warmth. He laughed at the way Daniel rolled his R's and laughingly told him to watch out for the girls who would, no doubt, fall for his beauty. When he told Daniel he would like to have a son like him he could not easily understand the boy's sudden expression of resentment.

The girls did look at Daniel in a special way and giggled when he blushed. They left a heart-pierced-with-arrow drawing on his desk once and though he tore it up furiously, he wondered whose heart it was. He was tanned in the summer and his muscles well developed, for then he could lift a stack of hay almost alone. He learned to drive a tractor and discovered Victor Hugo and Dickens at the same time and, as for inner life, there seemed to be an undisturbed process of grasping things, digesting them and projecting, in a relaxed way, peace and stability.

*　*　*

Daniel was back in the main street now and walking towards his flat. The hospital was dimly lit – corridor lights – and the sand ground under his sandals produced a pleasant summery sound. Desert nights are cold and he wondered if Haim Kalinsky was well covered. Are you cold Kalinsky? You can ask the nurse for a blanket, the way Yoram did, except that Yoram's chill could not be warmed by blankets, there was no blood left in him.

You died on that winter day Kalinsky. You took Shmuel with you and you died for me and now you are dying again and perhaps all that happened in between doesn't matter. Did you ever, do you still, think or believe that I forgot your choice? Not your fault, father. Who could face a decision like that? And had you taken me and left Shmuel, and had I survived then, would I have forgiven your ability to choose? I owe you my life because you let them fool you.

The second window from the corner was open. The white curtain swayed lightly and looked like angel's wings. The dark foliage of the cypress tree had a priestly quality and there was light in his own window.

Rina must be back for the week-end, he thought, which reminded him that he had promised to take care of Miriam's little boy and he was not sure he was looking forward to it. The thought of entering the room and enjoying the solitude of the half-empty flat vanished now. He walked once again around the block and when facing the

29

door tapped gently on it to be let in by a smiling vivacious woman.

If there was anything Rina did not contribute to the little flat, it was femininity. Her high dusty boots seemed to catch his eye wherever he looked though there were only two of them. A rucksack lay open in the middle of the room spilling out a collection of pottery sherds and the shirts she washed and hung to dry were old army shirts. She was bare-footed and wore khaki shorts which emphasized long thin legs covered with light hairs and bruises. Her T-shirt, clean and white, outlined tiny breasts but her long tanned hands ended in delicate thin fingers. She was two years younger than he was but moved with the swift gaiety of a teen-ager. Her face was covered with freckles which matched her red short-cropped hair – a crown of fire.

They shook hands and she remembered the kettle had been on – for hours – and when she went into the kitchen he found himself smiling. He was about to sit on the bed when she screamed, ' Don't sit!', and he noticed the large towel on top of the bedspread. Under it were more sherds and he pulled the small chair from the bathroom stepping on bits of clothing and equipment which seemed now to be cluttering the empty places he had enjoyed so much, including the second previously empty room. In the empty room a sleeping-bag was laid on the floor and next to it, in a vase, a bunch of desert plants only slightly revived from a long journey.

She poured tea in glasses and brusquely demanded, ' Well, what is it all about? Are you in love with a southern beauty? ' In spite of the answer he was about to give, he had to smile.

' No, it's my father. He's very sick.'

' I didn't know you saw him.' She was suddenly serious.

' I haven't yet, and not for a long time before now, but I thought I'd better be here.'

' Where is he? '

' Across the road. Second window from the corner.'

' Is he dying? ' She did not know how to pretend or play-act but the tone of her voice indicated the gentleness lacking in the way she phrased her question.

' I think so. What have you been up to? '

' Nabataeans again. The professor is going crazy with his new finds so he stayed near the dig. I'll go back to-morrow night. My God, how beautiful the things we found are. Is it cancer? '

' Yes, in the lungs. Do you have an extra sheet? '

*   *   *

As he was never faced with other choices, Daniel accepted Kibbutz life without pausing to wonder. He had nothing before, and everything now, and he was conditioned to fit into this structure. He visited cities several times, always with his school-mates, and it never occurred to him to wish another place was his home. His life was well planned by others – study and work and a few social duties – and if the lack of struggle in any way limited him, he did not know it. He was responsible for the school library at the age of fourteen and was given the pleasure of recommend-ing the books he devoured and loved to others and the joy of watching their grateful enthusiasm when they returned them. He was one of five Gilad children to enrol in the area high school and when he emerged first in his class in several subjects – though he had no parents who could be proud of him – several well-educated people in the Kibbutz shook his hand with an expression of pride. He was not particularly fond of farm work but during the hot harvest season he participated with the others, saving the after-work hours for long sessions with Tolstoy and Dostoyevsky.

At the age of fourteen he was found masturbating and had to face a talk with the local doctor who for some reason attributed it to Daniel's background rather than to his age. He was a year older than the rest of his class, and in school he met youngsters from other villages in the valley to discover how proud of and attached to Gilad he was. Were it not for a slight accent he could pass for a Sabra, and even this was not a goal but rather a fact in his life, and the surprise on faces caused by discovering he was an ' adopted child ' gave him neither satisfaction nor did it start him thinking. Several other adopted children grew very attached to one family or another and for them the adoption process was complete, but Daniel did not feel the lack of a family other than the large family of the Kibbutz as a whole, which satisfied his needs and left him alone. Once or twice a Jewish Agency woman came to visit Gilad to find out more about the children's background and once they had to go through the unpleasant process of looking at a collection of photographs trying, perhaps, to identify other members of their families.

Daniel claimed he knew his parents were dead and was excused from this session but he never indulged in self-pity about being an orphan. If he needed advice there was always the literature teacher in school, who encouraged and shared his enthusiasm for the Russian classics, or Yoram, who was not always there but still the closest person to Daniel – now in a more reserved shy way as the

32

gap between them was no more that between a child and an adult but rather an adolescent and a young man.

Yoram was a captain in the army, and although the war did not affect Gilad's children much, Yoram's participation in it involved Daniel in the way that the absence of most fathers involved their children.

Whenever Yoram came back – always hungry and tired and for a short hour – it was Daniel who shared his stories and, with a mixture of anxiety and envy, watched him mount the jeep and disappear behind a cloud of dust along the field track leading to the area's headquarters. Yoram's parents would have preferred to see a girl next to their son, but it was always Daniel – who was taller than Yoram now – walking the Kibbutz pavements with him, drinking in thirstily the vivid descriptions of battles and victories.

The war was over and Daniel was fifteen – the question marks in the file were forgotten by then – and Yoram decided, with the Kibbutz' permission after a long debate, to stay in the army for a few years. Daniel resumed his studies and the fact that he was now a citizen of the independent state of Israel did not change his routine – the trip on the tractor to school, studies, the walk back through the fields along the river and farm work alternating with library supervision in the afternoons, homework in the evening. He still shared a room with the same three boys, though Rivka was no longer in charge of them, and he still enjoyed the comfort of friendly books about distant worlds before going to sleep. The insolent penetrating smell of jasmin and the touch of dew-covered golden oranges had their effect and if Daniel were to ask himself where his home was – which he never did – he would naturally point to the silhouette of the water-tower of Gilad and to the little house covered with purple bougainvillaea where he had a bed, a desk and a cupboard.

In school he met Rina who lived in a neighbouring village. Other girls attracted him and he watched them with wondering eyes. He wondered whether their brassières hurt them. He knew their hair felt different and softer and he was frightened by their secret giggles. Two girls from town attended lessons and he liked their frilly blouses and flowery summer dresses and when he occasionally came across young lovers on the river banks he blushed with the knowledge that one day he would be doing the same.

Rina liked the same books. She saw him walking to Gilad one day with a book in his hand, a Gorky, and her laughter made him turn.

' You look like a drunkard from the back walking in zig-zags,' she said. He gave her books from the library and during breaks in the lessons they dreamt aloud about what was written in them.

' Do you remember when Sonia . . . Who is your favourite, Alexei or Pierre? ' It never occurred to him to talk to her about anything else, and with youthful haste they crossed together the Volga sunsets and Russian battle fields discovering with breathless speed more and more and over again.

One afternoon, walking together a part of the way – to the crossroad where he turned left to Gilad and she took the road to Shimron, she talked less.

' Anything the matter? ' Her freckled face lit now.

' Yes, I have to ask you something. I think of you and I see Grisha and the Dnieper and I hear your voice talking about books and you are not really there – you are here, in Gilad, and you are not really here either.'

' You sound confused,' he evaded.

' Well, it's just that I don't know anything about you, Daniel, the person. Nobody does.'

' What's there to know? You see me, we talk, we laugh, we study, what more? '

' I mean you. Who are you and what do you feel and what do you want? It's as if everybody has three dimensions and you have two – two neat and graceful and polite dimensions.' They had reached the crossroad now.

' It will rain,' he muttered, ' you'd better hurry.'

' I'll ask you again and again,' she said and walked away.

A truck driver going to Gilad gave him a lift and he found himself talking about grapefruit orchards just when the first drops of rain tapped on the tin cab of the truck. The smell of wet black soil filled his nostrils as winter clouds gathered above the valley in their welcome dark gray.

She did ask him again. He avoided her for a few days making sure he was in company of other Gilad students whenever walking home. The next time they were alone there was silence and she started.

' I'm not just curious, I have to know.'

He shrugged. The flame in her face joined the red hair.

' How many years have you been here? '

' Five, almost.'

' Tell me what it was like.'

' Where? '

' Before.'

' I don't remember.'

Was it aggression or impatience or disbelief in her voice?

' That's impossible,' she said. ' I remember things that happened when I was four and six and eight, you want to hide them.'

Did he want to hide anything? he thought. Not really.

'Do you remember your mother?'

'She was beautiful.'

'Were you an only child?'

'I had a brother, two years older.'

The road was muddy and the rubber boots felt heavy but the air was clean and fresh, making its way into the lungs effortlessly.

'What was he like, your brother?'

'He played the piano.'

'Tell me about your house.'

'I don't remember. It had a wooden floor and we could see the snow through the window. I remember the snow. Why do you have to know all this?'

'Was your father nice?'

'My father. His name was Haim, I don't remember him well at all.'

'What did he look like?'

'Tall I think. Well-dressed.'

'My God,' she exclaimed. 'Don't you lie at night awake and imagine them? Invent them? Try and reconstruct? Don't you care?'

'Rina, they all died when I was six. What do you want me to do, go back and give myself a family I don't have?'

'Do you think he was blond? Your father, like you?' There was a spark in her eyes now, she was almost playing a game.

'He could have been. He wore a hat most of the time, I think.'

There were flowers in the barley field – red spotting the young green grass.

'I think he was tall and blond, and had your gray eyes. He must have been very elegant and cultured and soft-spoken and he loved you very much.'

' All right,' Daniel accepted. ' So he was. If you read some more novels you'll be able to tell me more about him.'

The blessed crossroad appeared.

' I'll come over tomorrow. You said I should meet Yoram,' she mentioned.

' Sometimes he doesn't come home on Saturday.'

' I'll come over anyway.'

So she will, he thought, noticing her funny walk as she struggled with the sticky mud.

Rina had scratched the surface and reached the soft flesh he cared not to expose, or to admit was there at all. He was a tall blond elegant man, his father, she told him and Daniel could hear the piano notes played by Shmuel. It was Friday afternoon and Yoram's jeep came to a halt just behind him which made him jerk, then smile and climb up.

' So you've chosen a red-head,' Yoram said.

' Just a friend from school. She lives in Shimron.'

' Good-looking, too.'

' I don't think so. She's coming tomorrow, you'll see. She talks too much.'

On Friday nights the Kibbutz was turned into a large family. The tables in the dining room were covered with white table-cloths and two candles were lit to welcome the sabbath. The men wore clean white shirts which emphasized the ruggedness of their skin and after dinner, when the smallest children were put to bed, Yoram played the accordion and a few couples perspired dancing a polka. Daniel could dance but seldom did, because he would rather sit and watch Yoram's stubby fingers tapping the keys. It was raining outside and he figured Rina would not come if the mud was deep. Somewhere between the feet dancing the Horah and the sound of thunder a tall fair man was taking shape, subtle and permanent.

Rina arrived towards noon, holding an enormous bouquet of narcissus, drunk with their aroma. She was all laughter and joy and red hair and mud and chatter and, ignoring curious looks from several people, he took her to Yoram's room.

' Yoram, this is Rina.'

' At last,' she exclaimed. ' I didn't believe you really existed to judge by the way Daniel talks about you.'

Their laughter matched and for a moment Daniel was left out of it, but they went together to watch the river, which was strong and muddy now.

' Like the Vistula in Warsaw,' she said, looking at Daniel.

' I don't remember,' he answered and Yoram smiled and added, ' Just like the Jordan in winter, genuine and unique.' He took in Daniel's look of gratitude.

Yoram drove Rina to Shimron and Daniel saw him later that night in the dining room. They walked together along the pavement and Daniel sensed Yoram wanted to ask him something.

' She told me about your father,' he said.

' She doesn't know anything about my father. Neither do I.'

' She said, " supposing he was alive ".'

' He's dead. My mother and brother are dead. What's it all about? What are you trying to do? '

' Nothing, don't get excited. People who were thought dead show up sometimes. After all there were no name-lists in the gas chambers. Perhaps one should never lose hope.'

38

' And go around stopping people asking, " say, did you happen to have a son called Daniel who thought you were dead for the last ten years? ".'

' You know what I'm talking about. She finds it strange that you don't even try to find out, the way most people do.'

' Why doesn't he try and find out about me if he is alive? '

' Perhaps he is trying. I'm sorry, I would never have talked about it if it weren't for Rina. Sensitive girl, very affectionate.'

' She has no right to be so inquisitive. I met you in Bari and you brought me here. I'm happy with things as they are and what I don't remember I don't want to imagine.'

They never mentioned it again, neither did Rina, except once when Daniel graduated from school she said, ' If your father were alive he would have been very proud of you.'

Chapter Three

She insisted she would be the one to use the sleeping-bag and knowing how stubborn she was there was no choice but to give in.

' Do you mind if I move it to the bedroom? '

He was lying on the bed and next to the bed on the floor Rina was sitting talking about the Nabataeans. She described Petra, their capital, as if she had been there often and talked about their king – Harithath – as if she were in the habit of lunching with him daily. Petra was in Jordan, inaccessible, and Harithath ruled in the first century after Christ and he envied her imagination turning every piece of pottery into a usable dish and every ancient stone into a complete untouched castle. Rina was a graduate of the Faculty of Archaeology in Jerusalem but there was nothing scholarly in her approach to excavation or to history. Anything that was dated chalcolithic must have been used personally by Abraham, and in Iron Age sites King David camped – in all of them. She would have displayed very little surprise if at night an ancient figure were to emerge from the ruins on a site, and if this sense of continuity did not make her a better archaeologist, it added to the enthusiasm with which she joined any mission that set out for field work. Before she fell asleep she asked him if he wanted to talk about his father and when he said no she mumbled something about the Euphrates Valley and he could sense her soft breath across the room.

His thoughts wandered from Rina to Kalinsky across the road, to Lipsky downstairs and the doctor in the bar. Rina was now walking in Petra, the red rock city, or along a street in Avdat. She was conquering Damascus and Coele-Syria with Harithath or writing love letters in Aramaic. Kalinsky was in Jerusalem Avenue or wandering along Cracow Boulevard – did he stop at the Holy Cross Church to see Chopin's heart or did he not enter churches? And Lipsky with his wife clad in fur – she often mourned this famous fur coat – necking on the banks of the Dimbovita, shopping in the Calea Victoriei or Balescu Avenue. Is that what they dreamed of? Did Wadi Beer-Sheba enter their dreams, and Herzel Street and Minarets? Did the doctor dream of amputated limbs dancing alone or did he too have streets with foreign names forming a labyrinth in his subconscious? Daniel never dreamed, and if he did he never remembered his dreams, and again he thought of the child whose name he forgot who would stay with him the following day. He should ask Miriam what the child liked to eat and was there a date on which the death of Kalinsky was to be expected.

When he woke up he noticed a sheet covering his body. The sleeping-bag had disappeared and unfamiliar voices reached him from the empty room. He slipped into his shorts and tip-toed to the bathroom. Standing in the door-way he could see Rina squatting next to the piled sherds and Miriam's boy building a strange tower made of jar handles. The boy looked up and without so much as smiling resumed his game. Rina went to make coffee and since there was nowhere to sit and he did not feel up to

41

straining his muscles and bending down, he remained there standing and from his height the boy looked tiny and distant.

' What are you building? '

' Can't you see? ' The boy answered without looking up.

Daniel went to the kitchen to ask Rina for the boy's name.

' Shmuel, didn't you know? They call him Shmulik.' She laughed. ' He's four. The son of your step-sister and the grandson of your father. Isn't he adorable? '

' Shmuel. Of course. Yes, he is adorable I suppose, aren't all children? '

' He calls you Uncle Daniel, which is hilarious. I promised him you'd take him for a walk, and to a restaurant to eat.'

' You did? Is he moving in? '

' Don't be horrible. You're to take him to the hospital around five.'

' I see, so my day is fully planned. Thank you.'

' Hostile today, my God. Have some coffee and a Lipsky cake. I hope you have your nephew's taste, he adored it.'

' Where does one take little boys for a walk in Beer-Sheba? '

' Anywhere. I have to go to the Museum and do some work, maybe he would like to ride a camel? '

' You're crazy. When will you be back? '

' After lunch. I'm late now. Be a good boy Shmulik.' She addressed the boy in the empty room and taking her rucksack full of Nabataean dreams she disappeared. In complete contrast to her stormy manner she shut the door in an unexpectedly gentle way.

He told the boy they were going out and when they reached the street Shmulik pushed his hand into Daniel's.

'You're a big boy. You don't have to hold my hand.'

'Mother said to,' he insisted. His hand was sticky with the remains of Lipsky's cake.

'Where would you like to go? '

'She said you'll take me to the camels.' 'She' must have been Rina.

'Mother doesn't let me ride a camel,' the boy volunteered.

'If mother doesn't let you, you cannot. We'll go on a walk and I'll buy you an ice-cream.'

Daniel found it difficult to adjust to the boy's steps, but carrying him in his arms would have looked silly he decided. He looked at the boy, who had his mother's features, and he thought he was too thin. He was dressed in blue and his thin hands were lost in the short sleeves. After a few blocks Shmulik stopped abruptly.

'I forgot my hat,' he declared.

'We'll be back before it gets too hot.'

'Mother said never to go out without a hat.'

It didn't matter really as long as the time passed somehow so they returned, and disposing of the boy on Lipsky's terrace, Daniel walked up slowly to look for the hat. Suppose he didn't return immediately, he thought. The boy was a good boy, he'd wait there on the terrace, perhaps Mrs Lipsky would give him another cake and he would join them later. He looked through the window. Shmuel was alone on the terrace looking at the house's entrance impatiently. Daniel took the blue hat and walked down. It was too large for Shmuel's head and his ears stuck out under it as if supporting it.

'Grandpa Haim is in hospital,' he stated. 'Does he play doctor there? '

'He is sick, your grandfather.'

'My mother is in hospital, and my father, and my grandmother.' He talked with the pace of his own steps, stopping in the middle of words which Daniel wanted to complete for him. There were no buses on Saturday and Daniel decided that they should return by taxi. When they reached the centre of town the boy seemed tired. It was a long walk for him and the sun was scorching. His face looked red under the blue hat.

' Are you feeling well? '

' Yes, Uncle Daniel. Now I want to play.'

' I don't know any games. Here, let's have an ice-cream.'

They entered the crowded Eshel café on the main street and Daniel ordered two ice-creams. When the order arrived the boy pushed it away.

' Don't you like it? '

' I want real ice-cream, not in a glass.'

A short conversation discovered that the boy wanted a cone which resulted in a dripping mess on his clean shirt and a large smile.

' I will have a sister soon,' Shmuel said, now feeling familiar and comfortable. ' Do you have a sister? '

' No. What would you like to do now? '

' Now we play, then we see the camels, then we play . . . '

' Aren't you hungry? '

' I want a chewing gum.'

They stopped near a kiosk where he lifted the boy so he could choose from a variety of displayed sweets.

' This, and this, and this, and chocolate.'

He stuffed his pockets with the sweets and suddenly, in a street crowded with Saturday strollers, said mischievously, ' Catch me!', and turned to run, laughing.

Daniel caught up with him pushing several people on

the way.

'You want to play again? Not this game. Not in the main street. We'll go to eat. Uncle Daniel is hungry.'

It had to be Morris's again. Instead of walking now Shmuel was hopping on one leg, another game, holding on to Daniel's large sweaty hand. He knows precisely what he is doing, Daniel was convinced. He knows it exasperates me and he plays the innocent. He squeezed the little hand tight.

'That hurts,' Shmuel said, smiling.

'Stop hopping, it's impossible to walk with you.'

He was now behaving himself and with his free hand pulled the chewing gum in long cords out of his mouth, talking at the same time. They reached Morris's to realize it was too early for lunch and they were the only customers in the place. Daniel sat on the straw chair and looked at the Friday papers left on the table. The waitress – the same one, only her fingernails were painted red now – stood near them enjoying the boy's activities.

'The same,' he ordered, 'and chicken for the boy.'

'Your son?'

'No. My nephew.'

'He's cute. You look alike, he could have been your son.' Daniel turned to look at Shmulik. His profile was handsome and his body relaxed but still wiry and thin. He found no resemblance.

When they were through with the meal Daniel asked the waitress to call a taxi, paid the bill and led Shmuel out leaving behind most of the food, disarray of paper napkins, a filthy tablecloth and – which he remembered too late – Shmuel's blue hat.

They sat in the taxi and instantly Shmuel fell asleep, his head tilted to touch Daniel's shoulder. Daniel put his arm around the boy's thin shoulders and with a tinge of guilt pushed the boy's hair back from his forehead.

Rina could be seen in the window, seemingly waiting for them, and Daniel felt relief and fatigue. He carried the sleeping boy in his arms upstairs and placed him on the bed.

' What did you do to the poor thing? '

' What did he do to me, you should ask.'

' Come now, weren't you the same as a child? '

' I don't know. I hope not.'

' Have you never seen children in Gilad? '

' They were never left in my care.'

' Did you eat? '

' Sort of.'

' Well. You look exhausted. You can sleep on the sleeping bag. I have some work to do and then I am off until next Friday.'

' I doubt I shall be here next Friday.'

He fell asleep and when he opened his eyes he saw the child sitting on the floor all washed and combed looking at him. He smiled and the boy smiled back. The battle was over.

' I want to see my mother,' the boy suggested shyly.

' We'll soon go.'

Rina was packed to leave wearing her Arab headwear and boots and her empty bags dangling from her shoulder.

' The Nabataeans' Kingdom is awaiting me,' she declared.

' How are you going to get there? '

' The supplies' command car is in town, the driver came up to see his new baby girl. He named her Petra.'

' My God, poor child. I suppose you'll name your son Harithath!'

' A good Semitic name.'

Crazy woman, Daniel thought, and the three of them left the flat, each hopping on one leg down the stairs into the main road. Rina waved shalom and walked away and Daniel and Shmuel crossed the road to the hospital's entrance.

Near the gate Daniel stopped. He was looking for a nurse and couldn't see any. People were going in holding flowers they had bought a day earlier and an old man leaning on a cane asked Daniel some directions in Yiddish. The boy was restless and they entered the waiting room. Some of the patients were well enough to circulate and with a certain sense of superiority they discussed their ailments. Children were licking the chocolates rejected by their sick relatives and the sterile smell of disinfectant was now mixed with the cheap perfumes and deodorants of visitors. A couple of wheelchairs stood empty and gave Shmuel something to play with and Daniel walked over to the information desk where a white-haired red-faced nurse was patiently attending a young couple.

' He must be here,' they insisted.

' He's not on any of our lists. Did you try the private clinic? '

' He *is* here,' the woman said. ' Something must be wrong or you would tell us the truth.'

Her companion nodded in agreement and the nurse smiled at Daniel apologetically.

' Could he go under another name? ' she tried.

' Now, you see,' the woman was triumphant, ' something is fishy. Why would he go under another name? '

' I didn't say he did, or would. It happens sometimes.'
The man intervened now.

' Look,' he stated, ' Maya's uncle is in this hospital

47

somewhere. He had an attack of ulcers and we came all the way from Haifa. What's more, we have to return to Haifa tonight. He has been here four days. He is seventy and you don't just wander off at that age, so please tell us where he is or I shall go from room to room until I find out.'

Now the wife nodded and told the man to ask for the director. Daniel smiled. People were always asking for the directors as if they had access to mysterious truths, as if they provided final indisputable reliability. People liked to mention it later and say – giving themselves credit for infinite initiative – ' then we asked for the director of course, and naturally he helped us out '.

' Can I help you?' The nurse addressed Daniel.

' Can one of the nurses take a little boy to his mother who's visiting someone on the second floor? '

' Why don't you take him there, I don't see anybody around right now.'

' It's impossible for me to go up.' There was sadness in his face and the nurse did not ask more questions.

' I'll take him.' She told the couple she would be back in a moment and he called Shmuel who was sitting in a wheelchair.

' Kalinsky is the patient's name, it should be the room before the last one on the right. Shmuel, the nurse will take you to mother, tell her I could not come up.'

Shmuel was reluctant to leave his uncle and the wheelchair but followed the nurse up the stairs and Daniel left for the fresh dry air wondering if Maya's uncle would be on the list if he were dead. Lipsky's terrace was crowded now and he found a table in the corner and ordered some tea.

Across the street some of the people were treating their

visit to the hospital in a festive way, as if it were a social occasion. They dressed for it and the women were careful with their make-up – not too much but the right touch. Were they trying to cheer up the sick or were they reassuring themselves of their own well-being? On Lipsky's terrace were people who had just left the hospital – the relatives of the very sick never combined their visits with tea – and they were still discussing the various patients who had enjoyed their presence there.

' Of course I told him he looked better, but did you see his face? It used to be healthy, I mean – healthy – ' the thin woman emphasized. ' Skeleton. That's all that is left. Skeleton.'

' Well,' her friend sighed. 'You don't go and tell a man he looks like a skeleton. He'll be out next week, and off to the Trade-Union Sanatorium in the mountains, so that's lucky.'

' Lucky indeed, I shouldn't be so lucky myself.'

' Now why would they keep her in if they're not going to operate?' a teenage girl, wearing sunglasses, asked her father.

' Am I a doctor? '

And at another table:

' I told the doctor about the compresses. Just compresses and the right food and he would have been out by now.'

Old parents with a small suitcase were talking about their son. His leg had been amputated. What was there to say? Daniel thought. In the eyes of the woman he could see the two healthy legs of the young boy running naughtily down streets and the eyes of the father held the agony of one leg and a crutch forever. An ambulance sirened its way in and the people on the terrace looked at it knowingly, without panic or a shudder. They were all related to some sick person and thus allowed entry into the kingdom of doctors in white and nurses and laboratories. They lived with it around dinner tables asking for news and on the telephone repeating, ' a little better, thank you.' They knew the names of surgeons and medicines and once a week or every day they had breathed the hospital odour which still clung to their clothes. Mrs Lipsky was busy serving and giving advice and finding out. She knew most of the people, and she knew who they were worried about and she could talk about the doctors who frequented the Café Tikva and suggest, ' He is the best there is! ' or, ' I remember him back in Bucharest, you just have to trust him,' and Lipsky himself, always looking as if he were eagerly awaiting closing time, was considering whether or not to buy an espresso machine.

' Shall we go to the movies? ' the thin woman asked.

Her friend suggested cards and they asked for the bill. The girl wearing sunglasses was looking at Daniel, but he couldn't be sure because of the glasses. He too would go to the movies, he decided, and stood up to go.

It seemed that Rina's laughter still echoed in the empty flat and when he heard a knock on the door, he jumped up to open it.

It was Miriam. Alone.

' I am sorry to come like this. Are you alone? '

' Come in, it's all right. Where is the boy? '

' With my mother in the café. Would you like to come down? '

' How is he today? '

' He had pains at night. He doesn't look well at all. He asked about you and Shmuel told him you were here, I couldn't help it.'

Did he notice tears in her eyes?

50

There was helplessness. She was his half-sister, and he felt nothing. He did not want to put his arms around her shoulder and comfort her, and he almost felt sorry for himself for not wanting to. She was just another woman in the Café Tikva talking about a sick man and making the world seem like one large sterile hospital. She was just another woman wondering if her father would survive, wondering whether his doctor was the best, or did his best, whether there was anything she could do. Just another healthy woman, like the girl with sunglasses or the thin lady being caught in the labyrinth of Latin names and prescriptions and test results, regarding them as holy scriptures and through a relative exposing herself to a momentary proximity with the term ' End '.

' Look,' he fumbled, ' I owe you an explanation. I cannot do it. To tell you why I don't cross the road will mean telling you other things, some of which I don't understand. Tell him I'm here for army duty. Tell him I had to go south for a few days and I shall visit him when I'm back.'

She resembled Shmulik now, with puzzled, accepting eyes. What could he tell her? Tell her about Yoram, tell her about a moment on a winter day in Poland, tell her of a dawn in Haifa port, tell her he had lost his father long ago, and it was her father who was dying now, tell her he would go to the movies that evening?

' Shmulik forgot his hat at Morris's,' he said. ' I'll collect it and give it to you.'

There were many things she wanted to tell him but she thanked him and left and like a spy behind the faded curtain he watched her wipe her nose and walk to the terrace and then down the street with her mother and her son.

Miriam was a simple woman, but there were many things she could have told Daniel. She had no right to, she felt, and never would, but he had chosen an easy and selfish way, a manner lacking responsibility or maturity and she knew that he had avoided compromises and difficulties and unpleasant moments by imposing them unintentionally on others. A cruel thought crossed her mind as she squeezed Shmulik's hand by way of answering a question he asked. Daniel was playing a game. He was an in-between man, shedding the sensitivity of a Warsaw boy and not quite acquiring the toughness and frankness of a Gilad boy, out of choice, she thought, seeking comfort. Her mother was not silent about it.

'His own father,' she said. 'Very, very sick and not even one visit. That's what I always say, the communists in the Kibbutz have no respect, what can you expect if they don't live with their own children, cook for them, mend their socks, nurse them. Well, God bless her soul, his mother is lucky not to live to see such behaviour.'

'Mother,' Miriam hushed her.

'And after all Haim has been through, not to have at least the comfort of a loving son.' Dora Kalinsky, Haim's second wife, was a large woman. Her double chin and wrinkled neck betrayed at least fifty-five years and her gray hair was cut short and straight. She suffered from varicose veins and having to wear elastic socks did not make life in the searing heat any pleasanter.

'What did he say to you? He must have said something.'

'He said he will visit him one of these days. Mother, there is nothing more to say about it, leave him alone.'

'I'm not worried about him, it's my poor Haim, turning the world upside-down to discover this son of his, and offering him a house, and now . . .'

She stopped in the middle of the sentence as if suddenly realizing it was all beyond her.

Another desert sunset, with huge red fingers grabbing the sky and relinquishing it with a faint mauve gesture. Sabbath, the queen, makes an exit with the appearance of the first three stars gowned with memories of a restful day and another cycle begins as the fourth and fifth stars join the three, another seven days of toil and dust and perspiring underarms and tourist buses and army jeeps.

Daniel missed Gilad on Saturday evenings. It was a family day on the Kibbutz and he enjoyed watching parents seriously respond to the children's queries strolling along pavements all ending on the lawn in front of the dining room. He used to lie on his back on the grass and watch the light change the tree tops from green to a dark gray and then black and he even enjoyed the smell of the mosquito repellent he rubbed his arms and neck with. Next to him was Yoram, white shirt replacing his usual khaki, and later Rina, and they were making plans. He missed Gilad and he counted the months that had elapsed meaninglessly between the day he left the Kibbutz and now. Luminous multitudes of stars brightened the sky above Gilad and Beer-Sheba and the years were lost in a long count of Saturday nights. They were planning their future then and before he was seventeen he never asked himself what his life should be like. The future he dreamed about then held everything that his present state lacked.

The air-conditioned darkness engulfed him as he found an aisle seat in the large cinema. On the wide screen a happy family was obviously enjoying the advertised soup. A child had the whitest teeth because he used Shemen toothpaste and all the difficulties were removed from the life of a glamorous housewife once she acquired an Amcor washing-machine. The audience fidgeted impatiently, having seen the child, the housewife and the family so many times before, but Daniel seemed to enjoy it all. The film had good people and bad people and the bad were rather sympathetic but the good ones won and staying in his seat awhile when the lights were on at the end he was asked to leave by the usherette before the second show began.

When he walked by the Eshel restaurant he saw through the glass door the young army doctor eating alone and reading a book. He walked in and said shalom and accepted the invitation to join him.

' How is your friend? ' the doctor asked him.

' The same.'

' Lung, wasn't it? Did they do all the tests? Is it certain? '

He asked the doctor about tests, about chances of mistakes, about pain.

' Two healthy people talking about pain, what do we know? ' And he was telling Daniel about a brave young patient.

' I ask them if it hurts. They say yes and I nod as if I knew what it felt like. I don't really know pain. I can guess and imagine and take the little pain I have and multiply it but it's not the same.'

' Do you amputate, doctor? '

The doctor was eating roast chicken, a wing. He looked at it as if it had to do with the question.

' Yes. I have to. Needless to say, it's not my favourite surgical experience.'

' Don't you become immune after a while, say after the hundredth leg, doesn't it become just a piece of flesh which has to be separated from another, an independent bone to be sliced and sawed? '

' Not when you have to see the patient the next morning. Not even when it has to do with a malignant tumour and you know you are saving a life by amputating. Why these questions?'

' Just so. I had a friend. His legs were amputated and he died the same day and I thought he would have been better off dying with his legs, silly, I know. The myth of wholeness of the body.'

The doctor did not find a suitable remark to add to the story.

' Have you just been to the movies? '

' Yes. Across the street.'

' Any good? '

' Nothing special.'

A girl on high heels entered the restaurant. She walked to their table and was introduced to Daniel as Ruthy. Her legs were fat and hairy but her plump face reflected amusement and kindness. Her hair was tied back and her V-neck cotton dress proudly exposed the slopes of her round soft breasts.

' We go?' she asked, and explained to Daniel that they were going to the movies.

The doctor looked boyish now. He wiped his mouth quickly and fumbled in his pocket for money and keys. The girl excited him and he was shy with her and although he did not touch her there was something very sensual in the way he opened the door for her. Daniel remained there until the movement of people outside receded. He was jealous of the doctor and he smiled at the thought. Since Nili left him on a spring day in a room in Tel-Aviv, he had not thought of women's breasts. He envied the doctor's shyness. His hand, which was steady and strong in the rubber glove making an incision, was probably clumsy and hesitant touching Ruthy's skin.

He was thinking of Kalinsky's tests looking again at the window – standing now in his own flat realizing it was too early to go to sleep.

What do they do with the tissue they extract Kalinsky? After the biopsy, do they keep it in the lab so that it continues to live on after you? Do they burn it the way they burned witches and prophets? Will the X-rays be on file when you are gone, so we can add them to the family album as ' the last photograph taken of our father before he died '? The doctor said they tested bronchial secretions, he was eating while he told me but that was my fault – I asked him. I am your son and if I cough now it will be clean and healthy, and one day you began to cough and there were the germs of death in what you spat out. You never believed in God, did you? Not even on holidays when we went to Synagogue. You didn't lie to me and when I asked you if you were praying you told me you were reciting a Mickiewicz poem. Is that what you do now when you are in pain, or do you learn to pray? Do you pray for it all to end or do you pray to God to renew your life? Perhaps this is the only thing I really want to ask you.

The doctor, Daniel imagined, was not really watching the film. He was holding Ruthy and breathing in the freshness of her hair and neck. Tomorrow it would be the smell of ether and a mask on his face, the smell of talcum on his hands before he slips on the gloves, the smell of blood. Now he squeezes her shoulder and it responds, alive. What do they do with the limbs they cut off? Do they bury them, burn them, keep them in jars, use them for experiments, ask the patients whether they want them as souvenirs?

Sound is amplified on desert nights. Did he imagine he heard coughing from the hospital? Sleep father, sleep. An aria on a neighbour's radio, Othello. Nili loved jazz, she said when they first met. He loved opera. The cough stopped and the aria came to an end and silence resumed. They asked me – 'Suppose he is alive, Kalinsky ' – and the tall blond man entered my life. I let him in because he was dead, he was a dream, he was my creation and I could live with him or dispose of him. They were truly concerned, and Rina wanted to write letters and find out more. Did they envy my pastlessness? Did they want me to be an equal, with memories of a house and home cooking and a reproduction on the wall? She once asked me if I were ever spanked and I could not remember. I should ask you when I see you, did you ever slap my face? When they planted the doubt in my mind, do you know what my first thought was? Suppose mother did not die, I thought, and while Rina described to me the elegant tall man, I was reconstructing a beautiful woman who was my mother. I knew you to be dead and I hoped she were alive.

Chapter Four

Haim Kalinsky had never been a tall blond man. He was of average height and looks and habits and temper. He displayed neither particular talent nor ambition and when his parents decided he should attend university he consented and even acquired a mild taste for poetry and literature in which class he met the girl who was to be his wife later. He joined his father's business which was a small firm handling imports from Germany. He was not a lazy man and when his father died – of a heart attack during his sleep – he took over and doubled the turnover, married Mina and had two sons. Routine dominated his life, and if he could not remember any moments of hilarious laughter and joy, neither could he complain of great sorrows. He was considered an honest man, and was never faced with the necessity to lie or cheat to test this opinion. He was not a pillar of the community, he was kind to the poor and to the Synagogue but his own soul needed very little in the way of ceremony and at times he even thought he would rather his boys spoke Polish than Yiddish. A few years before the war he managed to buy a new house and not being a sentimental man he was not sorry to leave his father's house which was too small and rather old-fashioned. Zion was associated in his mind with several stories in the Bible, heat and flies and a good friend who left Warsaw and became a farmer there.

When war broke out he made vague plans to move his family to one of the villages where he had customers but on the first of October Hitler entered Warsaw and events moved swiftly which made him realize his inability to cope with quick decisions. He buried some gold in the garden before being moved to the Ghetto and when his wife was taken away he resigned himself to his fate, being helped somewhat by the knowledge that he was sharing it with hundreds of thousands which made him feel somehow safer.

On a winter day, in the camp, when he was told to choose between his two sons he experienced agony for the first time – he was still digesting the loss of his wife, a loss unclear and mingled with self-pity and remote hope – and his actions on that day were motivated in a way unknown to him. He could never explain why he clasped Shmuel to him and let them lead Daniel away. Were he asked in his Warsaw house to give up one of his sons he would never have been able to decide or to face the choice. There, in the snow, things just happened and he dared not look back, or cry out, or think. Two months earlier the hearts of his sons were replaced by yellow badges and they looked like so many other lambs to be slaughtered. A few days later, they came for the children and he noticed they took the boys who sobbed. He put his trembling palm to Shmuel's mouth and whispered to him to keep quiet. He covered his son with his weak body and a strange sensation of gentle love and dependence flooded him when he touched the thin limbs. He had never before fondled his sons, nor had he spanked them. It was their mother who had bestowed upon them both kisses and slaps. They left

Shmuel with him that night and when he had to share his own portion of bread with the hungry boy he wanted Daniel to be there, and somehow the loss of the young boy settled in him like a physical pain, a numbness at the edges of nerves which were hungry now for the tuft of blond hair.

For Shmuel he did fight. He offered his own life instead and for a moment it seemed that no human force could unclasp Haim's embracing arms. Shmuel did not cry, he trembled violently and the tears gathered in his eyes and when they took him away Haim was still embracing the cold narrow emptiness which had been filled with the young body. Someone told him to pray and he uttered a curse, thus cursing and weeping for the first time since he was a young child, and his tears were the lonely tears of an orphan rather than those of a bereaved father.

He was taken to another camp where definite news of his wife's death was merely a confirmation which did not result in a new wave of mourning.

How some people survived the war, what it was that made them be among the elected to live while millions evaporated in the darkest of smoke that covered Europe, is a divine riddle. Haim worked hard, suffered silently, and time, which had stopped for him when Daniel was taken, resumed its count of seconds when one day it was all over and softly-pronounced Russian words were heard in the camp.

He followed the army of Marshal Rokossovsky and when Warsaw capitulated he set out to look for his house, which he found in ruins. The gold was still there but he reburied it and joined the groups of people looking for shelter, for food, for firewood, for a piece of clothing, for a sign from somewhere that life was really to resume its old pace and acquire the meaning and content it used to have.

Dora Wishnevsky was working in a soup kitchen and managed to find a room in a half-destroyed house. A wall was missing and she was helped by some men who managed to reconstruct one from plywood. She was allowed to take home some left-overs from the kitchen and one day when Haim could not pay for soup she asked him to her room for dinner. She was never married and being rather unattractive she had given up all thoughts of a companion. That night Haim stayed in the little room and when he was about to leave she suggested he might stay as long as he was looking for work. With the same gentle sense of duty that made him sleep with his wife, he found himself making love to Dora one night.

She thought he was asleep. The candle was put out and she sat there, a virgin were it not for the Germans, and watched the features of this stranger relax into sleep. He was sleeping on a mat on the floor and she watched him from her low bed. He shivered and pulled up the thin cover, exposing his feet to the cold. Suddenly she desired him. She slipped off her gown and not sensing the cold slid in next to him. He mumbled something and she took his hand and placed it on her warm breast feeling for his body with her hands. She did not speak and when he opened his eyes he met her smile, which transformed her face. After he made love to her, he wanted her again, this time not with a remembrance of a forgotten sensation but with a new passion. Not with the rediscovery of his own body but with a sense of pleasure, a physical pleasure, new and mounting and explosive.

The little room never enjoyed the sun and only Dora's watch indicated the fact that a new day had begun. She dressed to go to work and he went to look for wood, looking forward to the night. They talked little. Their past lives were not mentioned and they each preferred to carry their own burden of the war years, a vacuum or a hunch separately. He did not kiss her when she entered the room, or stroke her hair or caress her skin as she moved about preparing a soup and slicing the bread. Only when the room was darkened and the outside with its painful scarred face was locked away he was thrown towards her, feeling as intensely ashamed of his desire as she felt proud of it.

When she told him she was pregnant he was relieved. His desire was no more a forbidden pleasure, it took a form he knew. It was acceptable and normal and he offered to marry her and told her about the gold in the yard.

Dora Wishnevsky and Haim Kalinsky were married by a Rabbi who frequented the soup-kitchen. She bought a cheap ring which he placed on her finger and she took the day off. It was the first spring after the war. The air was brisk and the Vistula flew by with vigour carrying with it some of the war memories. Children were allowed to cry now and people emerged every day from the ruins heroic and stubborn and hopeful to rebuild their erased city.

Haim took Dora to the Muranov quarter to the site of his old house. They dug out the gold and looked among the ruins.

' What were your children like? ' she asked for the first time.

' They were good children.'

' Do you want a son? '

He did not care, and towards the end of the summer Miriam was born. Miriam grew with the city, she learned

62

to talk as the last tuft of smoke from the crematoriums disappeared and she said, ' Mommy ', as the large grave-yard gradually gave way to the shaping new metropolis. Haim was working, in partnership with two others, and when Dora suspected he had something to do with the black market she did not mention it. They had two rooms now in a new block of flats, and food, and toys for the baby, and a few friends and a fresh layer of memories separated from other layers by sensations unmentioned, horrors untalked about, pain without details or shape and perhaps dreams forgotten with dawn.

Dora grew fat after she had Miriam, and Haim was losing his hair. The baby was pretty and joyous and Haim spent many hours talking to her and playing with her on the floor, something he never did with his sons.

They were not going to stay in Warsaw. The city gave them what it could, but it would never be home again and they were wondering whether to move to Germany, to go overseas to America where Dora had some relations or simply move to another town in Poland.

They applied to the communal service for advice and it was there that for the first time the idea of going to Israel was suggested. Haim wanted to go to Germany. There were opportunities there, he argued. They could save money and then go to America or Israel. At night, in bed, Dora spoke up. First gently and meekly, and then with strength and enthusiasm.

They should go to Israel, she said. Nothing else was safe, and Miriam could grow up without yellow clouds over her curly head. The country of oranges and prophets and freedom and sun. They had enough money to start and she could work too. She squeezed his hand as she talked and he knew she really wanted it and said he would find out more about it.

They went on living in Warsaw. Occasionally they referred to the possibility of leaving but Miriam was now
wearing a school uniform. They moved to a larger flat,
Haim was a partner in a few shops in town and there was
no hurry.

Rumours from Israel suggested that life was tough and
demanding and several people returned after a few years
and resettled in Poland, criticizing everything to do with
Israel in spite of the glee in their children's eyes whenever the name was mentioned.

One day a young man, well-dressed and smiling,
knocked on the door. The Kalinskys were having supper,
expecting a few friends to come in later for a card game.
The man introduced himself as a Jewish Agency clerk
and politely apologised for coming unannounced. Miriam,
whose best friend was a girl who had been to Israel for a
few months, watched him with admiring eyes and Haim
offered him a seat.

' I need some details about your previous family,' the
man explained. ' There are many reunions and relatives
find each other even after years of separation. If you
suspect any of your people are still alive, they might be
traced and found.'

' They are all dead. The ones I cared for.'

' Your wife is listed as dead, and this was verified. What
about the boys? '

' One was taken first. They said they would shoot him.
The other, Shmuel, was left with me for a while and was
taken later.'

He wanted to ask Miriam to leave the room, but did not
quite know how to do it.

' How old was the first one? '

64

'Six, Daniel.'

'Do you have a photograph of the boys?'

He had none. The young man figured Daniel should be about twenty-five now, and a photograph would not help much anyway.

'Were the boys born in Warsaw?'

'Yes.'

'What language did you speak at home?'

'Yiddish and Polish.'

'Did you ever think of going to Israel? We can help you, many people left and they are very happy there.'

'I know. We thought about it. But we are growing too old to start anew.'

'Do you mind if we try and find out about the boys? You never know.'

The young man told them several stories of meetings between parents and children, brothers, sisters . . . He was almost boasting when he talked, as if he had the power of a God to give people the unexpected, the greatest of joys, as if he were in charge of resurrections and the announcer of redemption.

Before he left Haim sighed.

'No use, they are all dead.' And the man looked at Miriam as if in her eyes he was to find the hope her father's lacked.

'Do I have brothers, father?' Miriam asked.

She went to sleep that night thinking of her two brothers, tanned and handsome and protective. How she wanted to have a brother! And Dora asked Haim if he believed there was a chance, and when he embraced her in the large bed he remembered Shmuel's body clinging to life.

'You're hurting me,' Dora whispered.

Suppose they are alive, he found himself thinking. Are they honest? Are they strong? What language do they speak? How tall are they? Would he recognize them? Do they know each other? And again, for a brief moment he was an orphan, a middle-aged orphan holding on to his fat comforting wife.

A few months later the young man from the agency knocked at the door.

*   *   *

Along the banks of the Vistula Warsaw was executing its motto, *Loutemnit Procellas,* while the Jordan flew south feeding green-blue fresh water to the Dead Sea. Daniel was lying on his back reading one day, when Stash, his Polish class-mate, burst into the room waving a letter. His face was red and he could not contain his excitement.

' Read it! '

It was a short letter. It simply said that there was a chance that members of Stash's family were alive and to be found. The agency needed several details to verify the connection and would he please send a resumé of all he remembered and a photograph. Daniel never cared much for Stash, who was a year younger. He did not care to share a past or a present with him, and he was rather surprised to be approached in such a passionate way with what for the boy was a cause for a tremendous excitement.

' Just write them. Do you remember a great deal? '

' Not really. I had a sister, an older sister. She was blond, like you. I had a large green car. My sister's name was Katia. They left us with a farmer away from town and I cried, then she went away with a nun dressed in gray.'

' You can write all that. Do you have a photograph? '

' Only recent ones.'

Stash had pimples and wore glasses and Daniel wondered how he looked when he was four or five.

' Do you know the name of the village or the farmer? '

' No, but they would have it on file because I was taken straight from there to the train for Trieste and then to Bari.'

There was a sudden silence. Did Stash think Daniel was jealous? Daniel fumbled for his papers. When he looked up at the boy he noticed he was crying behind his glasses and he walked up to him and placed his hand on his neck where the auburn hair touched the blue shirt.

' They wouldn't write to you unless there was something definite,' he said, ' just write the letter and they'll answer soon. You should be happy.'

' I had a large green car, with front lights,' the boy mumbled sobbing and clasping the letter as if it were his mother, his sister, his toys, his father and his dreams he walked out of the room, towards the river.

Daniel was rather frightened and for a few days he found himself watching for the mail. He seldom received letters, never an official one and Yoram's messages arrived scribbled on the backs of funny postcards. Stash avoided him for a week but he did receive a reply asking him to come to Jerusalem.

Stash did not return for a few days and Daniel mentioned the episode to Rina.

' You see,' she said, ' I told you.'

She knew she was being tactless and she wasn't quite sure what she meant by, ' I told you.' Even if Stash had found a family – it didn't provide tall blond fathers to all the war's orphans.

When Stash returned he was not alone. A young woman

was with him, blond – the colour of Daniel's hair – and rather plump. He took her to Daniel in the dining room and said:

' My sister, Katia.'

The girl smiled and put her hand on her brother's shoulder. They talked awhile. Katia was the only one left of the large family. She had lived in Israel for several years now and was married. Stash was going to stay with her and perhaps leave Gilad and continue to study in Haifa.

' You will visit us,' she said to Daniel.

' Of course.' He watched them leave and when he walked to his room he saw them sitting on a bench talking and laughing.

What could he say to Shmuel if he found him, he wondered. Once they were in the same womb, then in the same house, shared the same toys and sat at the same table. There was nothing to say about that. Would he tell Shmuel about Yoram? Rina? Books he liked? The ache in his back when he harvested the grapes? His fear of snakes? His secret poems? Would he ask him if he remembered the day in the yard behind the barracks when someone decided which of them should live? He knew he could tell him all these, and other things as well as he knew that he was dead. They were all dead. Was he crying when he heard Katia's laughter in the dark?

Rina was now in the habit of listening to what is perhaps the most tragic radio programme in the world. Three times a week, just before the news broadcast, for five whole long minutes – ' Who recognizes, Who knows '. Names, dates of birth, places. Very dry, very boring to whoever is not interested. ' Mr Cohen of Baltimore looking for his nephew born in Minsk in 1933 to Ruth and Abraham

Mendel.' Each announcement is repeated twice. 'Mrs Nechama, née Balewitz, looking for her sister born in Odessa in 1909.' 'Mr Levy, from Salonika, looking for a younger Mr Levy son of Rachel and Shlomo . . . ' How many people listen every day, every week, for years? Perhaps – no, it is another Levy. Is there ever a face that lights up? The nephew of Mr Cohen, would he be a truck driver waiting for the news on his transistor radio on the way to Eilat? Does he brake and stop the truck? Does he hurry to a telephone? Suppose someone hears a name and knows the person is dead, would he tell? Is there ever a mistake in identity; so many Levys, so many Cohens, now grown up or pimply or with new names and foster parents. 'Left Zhashkov in 1885, left Berlin in 1933, born Bernstein to Leah and David.' His brother in Montreal, her aunt in Sydney, in Jerusalem, in Manchester. Every week, a new jig-saw puzzle made up of sound waves with a clean dry voice that ploughs hearts and minds, and sows hopes.

One day Rina heard it. It was short and clear. 'The family of Daniel and Shmuel Kalinsky from Warsaw is looking for information concerning them.' It was repeated twice and she wished they would go on repeating the names and the words. How could she tell him? She walked to Gilad, reaching it by nightfall, and was told that Daniel was working in the cowshed. Does one just go and say, 'Your family is looking for you?' Would they take him away, she wondered and for a brief moment she wanted to harbour the secret and never share him with this new unknown family. He turned to her with a worried look. Perhaps he knew when he looked at her. She avoided his eyes and was unable to speak. He put the spade down, took his shirt and walked to the tap in the yard. He let the water stream down his neck and back and shook bits of dry manure from his sandals.

'Let's go,' he said, placing a wet clean hand on her shoulder.

'I have to tell you something.'

'Not here, you're shivering.'

'I ran all the way.'

They walked in silence towards his room when she stopped abruptly.

'Look Daniel, let's not play games. I listened to the radio. Your family is looking for you. And for your brother. They're in Warsaw.'

'Did they say family?'

'Yes. What are you going to do?'

'Take a shower,' he grumbled.

She wondered whether to leave him alone or stay and help. Help with what? He was a grown-up man. His muscles moved gracefully when he lifted stacks of hay and his eyes held no sadness. He was not troubled, he was easy and gentle and if he did not care more about the things around him, it was a result of security and not of detachment. What could she add? Hold his hand in hers – how she wanted to – and caress his golden brown skin – how she longed to – and prepare him to face something she knew nothing about. She had a father at home who was a farmer from the Ukraine, she had a mother who was a teacher. They were always there and when they were gone for a few days she was left with a sense of freedom and independence. She looked forward to her army service as it meant leaving home and what could she tell this man in front of her.

'I think I love you Daniel,' she said.

It was not dark yet, and birds settled on the pine

branches for the night. She did not mean to say it, but all she could see was his back, as she was walking behind him on the narrow pavement, and all she knew was that he was being taken from her, and her freckles burned deep brown in her cheeks. He did not turn to look and she knew he heard her. When he turned to her, opposite his room, she was gone.

The first thought that passed through his mind was that Yoram was away on manoeuvres and would not return before Saturday night. There could, of course, be other Kalinskys, other Daniels too, and why would they use the radio, they must have had his name on file somewhere, they could have written him a letter. He thought of Stash, who had left Gilad for good. He entered the room. One of his room-mates was asleep and Daniel tiptoed to his cupboard to get a towel and a change of clothes.

He wished he could stand there under the cold shower for ever. The water parted his hair in the middle and he closed his eyes. The drops slid down his chest and along his arms to form a cool pool around his feet. His skin still retained the pleasant odour of cow manure and August sweat and the coarse soap gradually neutralized it. A desire for Rina flushed through him momentarily as he could hear her voice again but he relaxed until the voice of a friend suggested he had been using the shower for too long. It was the end of a long summer. School was over and he would join the service in two months. It was a summer of work and excursions and a good harvest. A summer of good books and no plans and little to worry about, and he was standing now in a pool of soapy water drying himself knowing he was not alone. Somewhere in Warsaw there was a family looking for him.

He flung the wet towel over his shoulder and combed

71

his hair. The night was hot and humid and the frog song monotonous and consoling. People said good evening to him, someone asked for the time, the dining room lights seemed too bright from the distance and two girls in shorts were giggling. His room was empty now and the bed inviting. He put off the lights and opened the window and the door. Green smells infiltrated the room and he lay on his back. Somehow the air above his chest felt heavy. He had an identity, a commitment, a past, a future – it was all in the humid air weighing him down. He imagined his mother approaching and he was four or five again, and shamelessly he burst into tears. He was frightened.

The next morning he wrote a letter to the agency. He wanted some details about his family; he wondered whether there was a chance that Shmuel was alive. He was very happy in Gilad and intended to make it his home but naturally he wanted to know what the chances were of meeting his family.

He showed the letter to the Kibbutz secretary who shook his hand warmly and seemed to be very happy for him. By the evening everybody was congratulating him and asking questions which he could not answer.

' Are they coming over? '

' Will you be going to Poland to bring them? '

' What does your father do? '

He wanted to be left alone but found himself walking towards Shimron. He felt guilty about Rina, and although her declaration of love puzzled and embarrassed him he wanted to see her.

Daniel was very fond of Rina. She was a mate, a friend, over-excitable but genuine. He could confide in her and she made him laugh. He was a virgin and when he thought of women they were different from Rina. He imagined them soft-skinned and perfumed. He wanted them dressed in frills and ruffles and the girls he grew up with were handsome and well-built but he was too familiar with them. Their skin had the quality of his own and their legs and underarms were hairy. He was never close to a girl, and his dreams were derived from books and films. He was vain about his looks and at times thought of going to town to one of those cafés which he knew they frequented. He was walking to Shimron now. His feet sank in the layer of dust on the road and he enjoyed the sight of heavy combines silhouetted against the sky awaiting the ignition and the action.

He reached the Moshav rather late and there was only one light in Rina's house. Her father's small car was not in front of the house and he assumed the light was in Rina's room and gently tapped on the half-closed shutter. It was flung open and the red hair appeared above curious eyes.

'You!' she exclaimed, and jumped out through the window.

'I was taking a walk. I owe you an apology. I'm all right now.'

'Did you write them?'

'I wrote to the Agency. I should have an answer in a few days.'

They sat on a pile of stuffed sacks. Rina opened a hole in one of them, let some chopped carobs out and munched them.

'I didn't know how to tell you. I must have made a fool of myself, but then, how do you deliver this kind of news?'

'You were all right. I'll adjust to the thought and that's all. After all, most people do have families.'

' Aren't you happy, somewhere inside you, you must have felt lonely at times, or jealous of others, or missing something.'

' The truth? ' He paused. She looked very young now. ' Yes I am quite happy. I never gave it much thought though, or missed it, I had friends you know, never alone.'

' Yoram,' she sighed. ' Well, you are both going to be in uniform now, so the gap is closing. He can't play father any more. Did you tell him? '

' He's away.'

' I am sorry about the other thing.' She put her thin long-fingered hand on his.

' I wish I could have given you something in return. I'm very fond of you and you're very young and I shall be gone in a month and you'll forget all about it. I am not very good when it comes to talking like this and I can't say what you want to hear.'

' Will you give me a gift? '

' Of course Rina.'

' Please kiss me.'

He knew that he was blushing. He took her head in his large hands and softly touched her. He felt her body move towards his and her lips opened. He could taste the carobs on her tongue and feel her teeth, and her hands pulled his head towards her. His eyes were open and he could see her face. She never looked prettier, or sadder, or less desirable to him. He felt ashamed and guilty and tenderly pushed her away.

' We shouldn't have done it. It doesn't mean anything.'

' I wanted it so much,' she said, now composed and smiling again.

' Just something to remember. You may forget it.' He was thirsty and they went in for some tea. He wished they hadn't gone in because in the light of the kitchen lamp she was a stranger. He kissed her and for a moment she gave him all that was in her, and now those long limbs and her curly hair moved about like rejected gifts.

On the day Yoram returned there was a letter in the mail for Daniel. He put it in his pocket and walked to the river bank when others dispersed for their afternoon sleep. It was in a square envelope and his name was typed on it. They were happy to notify him that his father was alive and well. His mother had died in the war and his father remarried and had a daughter. They lived in Warsaw where Kalinsky had a good job and the necessary steps were being taken to inform him of Daniel's whereabouts. Shmuel was taken away at the beginning of the war, and there was a slight chance that he might be alive somewhere. So the radio announcement would be repeated for a while.

In Latin letters followed an address in Warsaw and they suggested he write his father there. He could write in Hebrew and the Agency representative would translate it for the family. Was there anything they could do for him? They had discussed with Kalinsky the possibility of immigrating and he seemed to be considering it. If he wanted consultation the social worker handling the case would be at his service, any time. Then followed some warm words of congratulation and a woman's signature.

His mother was dead. He knew it was all wrong but what he wished he could do then was to take the letter and throw it to the river and forget the address on it and all that it meant. His heart was beating fast but his head felt empty of thought. The river was shallow and slow and it made its way to the lake, to continue south and die in the Dead Sea – a white majestic death of salt. That terrible moment which he had erased from his memory took shape again, and there they were – his father and Shmuel – walking away from him. Some instinct told him his brother was dead and though the day was unbearably hot he shivered. He replaced the letter neatly in the envelope and found a smooth surface under the trees. Ignoring the flies he fell asleep. When he opened his eyes Yoram was squatting next to him and by the look in his eyes Daniel knew he understood.

' Do you want to talk or would you rather not? ' Yoram asked, making himself comfortable on a severed trunk.

' Not much to say.' Daniel, when talking to Yoram, looked him straight in the eye, always. ' I feel terrible and the worse for feeling terrible. It's sudden, yet it isn't. The thought has crossed my mind often. What do I do next? '

' You act like a man. You have a new responsibility and you face it. You sit down and you write a loving letter and you find out more about your family and you arrange to meet them and if God or nature meant us to have families I dare say that everything will fall into place.'

' I don't know the man. My mother is dead, he's got a new family. I've never corresponded with strangers.' He felt it was too much, and smiled. ' I'm sorry, I'm being spoiled and harsh and difficult. You're right of course.'

They got up to go to the dining room. Yoram was talking, his hand on Daniel's shoulder.

' You resent the change. You had it comfortable and good and you didn't have to think. You're accepted here and it's a very small world and you didn't ever pause to think whether it fully satisfied you. I'm your friend, your brother, I know you well, but I've often wondered what would it take to pull you out of yourself and shake you up. Make you question things, assess yourself and your

76

life, decide what you want to do and how. Perhaps this is the moment and the push and you'll be grateful that it happened.'

'There will be two and a half years in uniform now, thank God.'

'You see, that's your attitude again. Another retreat, another way of life where things are decided for you and planned and thought out to the last detail. I hope you go to an officer training school, I would like to see you responsible for others. What about Rina?'

Daniel blushed, remembering her narrow lips.

'What about her?'

'She loves you, doesn't she?'

'She's young, and once I'm away she'll be all right.'

'Don't you feel anything for her?'

'Not that way,' he muttered.

They reached the lighted area. A movie was being shown outdoors and they joined a group of people carrying chairs. He sat on the lawn watching the sky rather than the screen, looking for Orion's sword and winking back to the Pole star. In his mind he was composing a letter to Kalinsky. Could he open it with – 'Dear Father?' As a child he called him Papa.

'Dear Father,' he wrote, 'you will understand me when I say that this is a very difficult letter to write. Of our life together I remember very little, and we have to find the courage and the love to start something new. Perhaps the knowledge of your being my father should suffice, but I have lived many years, happy years, with your absence, and I know you will fill the emptiness, I also know it will take time and effort.

'Where to start? It would be impossible to describe

77

the past years. I am now almost eighteen. I shall send you a photograph if you wish to have one. I live in a Kibbutz called Gilad. It is in the hot Jordan valley, near the river, and the land is fertile and yielding. I work on the farm when I don't study, and I shall be joining the army in a few weeks for two and a half years. I was always well taken care of by the people here, and was never made to feel an outsider. I graduated from school this year and if the Kibbutz makes it possible perhaps I will resume my studies. I read a great deal, mostly poetry these days, and I am healthy.'

He read the above and felt ridiculous. What would Kalinsky know about fertile soil, or the Jordan valley, or the poets he cared for. He knew warmth was expected of him, but warmth was not an abstract quality to be produced and floated off. He continued all the same.

' I understand you remarried and have a daughter. I should like to hear more about your family. Did you come across any people who saw mother before she died? When was Shmuel taken away from you – is there really any hope of finding him? I would like to think that you might consider leaving Poland to come to Israel. I shall try to make you feel at home here, it is a tough country, a wonderful one, and the only home one can take for granted.

' I live with three classmates in a comfortable room, we work eight hours a day now that school is over and the evenings are devoted to reading, cinema, theatre, music and just spending the time with friends. I have a friend here, a boy named Yoram. He is older than I am, is in the army and a native of Gilad. Everything that is good in me, and about my life, I owe to him.

78

' How old is your daughter? I am sure she would love it here, it is a paradise for children. As you see, I have forgotten Polish and Yiddish completely, and I shall have your letters translated. Do you live in our old house?

'Funny, a girl asked me if I was ever spanked by you, I could not remember.

Awaiting your letter,

Daniel.'

It had nothing to do with what he wanted to write. Perhaps he should have lied and told his father how happy he was, how often he thought of him all these years, how he was longing to fall into his arms. He did not feel anything, he did not want to commit himself more than he did and he was relieved when Yoram was not to be found. He sealed the letter, wrote the strange address on an airmail envelope and disposed of it as if it contained something contaminating. He felt free again, as if the act of writing settled the account, as if the letter was a final word, a heavy duty performed, and lying on his stomach, his hands supporting his head, he was engulfed again in his favourite book of Hebrew poems, carried with its images to elephants in the sky, lightning in cats' eyes and the rounded limbs of distant maidens.

Chapter Five

When Kalinsky opened the door and saw the young man smiling he knew immediately.

' May I come in?' the man asked.

Dora appeared in the kitchen doorway and then stood in front of him awaiting a verdict.

' I have a letter for you. Daniel is alive and well.'

' And Shmuel? '

' We don't know yet.'

Kalinsky did not hide his excitement. His hands were trembling as he opened the letter and he looked at the hand-writing for a few seconds before he realized it was in Hebrew.

' Shall I translate it for you? '

Miriam came in and sensing the importance of the moment held her mother's hand in silence. The young man's voice was deep and pleasant and every word he uttered while reading seemed to add a beam to a bridge. Across time – Dear Father – across countries – Gilad, Jordan, the valley – across hearts. When he finished Haim asked shyly if he would read it again, which he did. This time Kalinsky stopped him to ask questions and his smile was replaced by a compassionate look. He was participating, he was there, and the voice was that of his son.

They opened a bottle of vodka and raised their glasses and when the man left Haim took the letter and caressed it, telling Dora she needn't cry and repeating and memorizing the lines to Miriam. Late that night he wrote a letter to his son.

* * *

The last days of summer. A drying season in yellow and dust with bursting grapes and armies of flies. The valley is ploughed dark brown and the wind is the carrier of clouds if not yet of rain. Sweaters are spread on the lawn to air and some of the young girls begin to knit. The river is at its shallowest and the birds migrate south to warmer climates. When the letter reached Daniel he put it in his pocket and pretended to forget about it until the evening. It was written in Polish and there was only one man in the Kibbutz who could read it to him, the shoemaker. Daniel in all the years he had been there, exchanged perhaps six phrases with the man, and here he was, in his room, trusting him with this most personal thing. Zvi put his spectacles on and offered Daniel some coffee. They talked for a while about work, Daniel seemingly relaxed and patient. Zvi looked at the letter, nodded to suggest he understood the handwriting and in a rather amusing dramatic voice began to read, stopping every now and then as if unsure about a word, then resuming.

' My little boy,' it started,

' Is it your father's first letter? ' he asked, not looking up.

' Yes, I am sorry to trouble you,' Daniel added.

' Very interesting, very interesting,' Zvi murmured.

' So, my little boy. It will take many letters to tell

you all that happened to us since the war, or during it. Now that I know you are well and happy it doesn't matter really and we can look forward to the years to come. Unfortunately we learned about your mother's death from a woman who was with her to the end. She died of disease in a labour camp, not in the gas chambers.

'Shmuel was separated from me, the way you were. There was nothing I wouldn't have done, and nothing I could do to help it. I cannot believe I am actually writing to you, my Daniel, and you are sitting somewhere and reading it.

Zvi looked up at him, and Daniel motioned him to read on.

'Our old house was in ruins when I returned to Warsaw and with the help of Dora, your stepmother, we managed to face the hard years and once again I am working and relatively comfortable. Your sister Miriam goes to school. She keeps asking about you, please send us some pictures. The way I remember you does not help me to reconstruct the image of a young man. I heard about the Kibbutz resembling the Kolchoz, is that so? It is strange to think of you in the army, there was never a soldier called Kalinsky... There was never a farmer in the family either. I cannot offer you much right now, if we can save some money we shall come to visit and then decide about leaving Poland. Right now it is impossible. I used to read poetry when I was your age, it was then that I met your mother, may she rest in peace. I don't remember ever spanking you, I don't think I ever saw you cry either. I once spanked Shmuel because he hurt you. He used to play the piano beautifully. I seldom go to synagogue but I shall now, and offer a prayer of thanks. Please describe to me everything about your life, your friends, your village. Is the Jordan anything like the Vistula? Dora joins me in sending her love, so does little Miriam. I am a very happy man now, my son,

Your father.'

Daniel couldn't sleep. For a while he imagined the hospital ether and iodine odours invading his room sterilizing it, suffocating him, then he smiled. He had lived almost thirty years with his body, so many nights, and yet every night he moved and tossed and turned to find the best position for sleep. It was ridiculous, he thought, for a grown-up not to know whether he slept on his back, or side, and yet he did not. He realized he had taken off all his clothes before he fell asleep and when he stood up naked and walked to the window he felt he would like never to dress up again. He wondered whether the doctor was sleeping with his girl – surely not in the barracks where he lived – and flung the shutter open. Stars were disappearing fast and the moon not to be seen. The morning star bright and close threatened the arrival of another hot day and the light gray gave way to a cloudless pink horizon. In Gilad they are out in the fields he thought, and once again he remembered that he ought to get himself a new watch, it had been ten years since he lost it.

What are you dreaming about Kalinsky? He had a desire to cross the road and tip-toe through the silence and the whiteness and watch the man sleep. He remembered the first letter Kalinsky wrote him and the ones that followed. Nine years of letter-writing. Five happy ones and four of misery, every letter adding to the pattern: bits of information, little complaints, big expectations, at times a poetical line, more often, a pragmatic description of events.

I learned to know you Kalinsky. Your headaches and your rheumatic pains, your shop and the state of your affairs. I could almost understand your letters without a translation. You grew old in them, and your face wrinkled, you were losing your hair and your eyesight and you were evading my questions, evading issues, offering no comfort, remaining a detailed abstract. Rina said I would learn to love you through the letters. It never happened. Every letter substituted a drab reality for an illusion. Every line carried you away from me, until – when you were waiting for your visa to enable you to come – I hardly bothered to read them. You asked about the price of bread and vegetables and I wanted to tell you about almond trees in blossom. You wanted me to enquire about apartments and jobs and I did so saying always – a relative of mine – never my father. Yoram's parents suffered from malaria drying marshes when they were newcomers and you wanted me to find out about exchange rates. I wrote you back, Kalinsky. Do you have my letters? I sent you some photographs – you wrote and said they made you cry, I resembled my mother. We knew Shmuel was dead. Did you know all along? Did you feel it in your knees and guts one day, the way people do?

You read about the border clashes and you wrote me worried letters, you lost me once, you said, and you could not bear to lose me again, not realizing that when you lost me in the back yard and I was six, it was forever even if my ghost met you in the port of Haifa so many years later. Miriam's letters touched me, she had pride, Dora's letters had warmth and curiosity and yours were screaming a need, many needs, and fear, many fears, and I could not answer the need nor calm the fear.

The morning star disappeared. On the hill a few camels were grazing elegantly, swaying long necks and merging with the colour of the dunes turned gold with the first light of day. Daniel was tired and the room was cold and the night nurses left the hospital now looking neat and fresh.

Our letters never touched, never crossed, Daniel thought. We took parallel roads and when circumstances made them meet – they refused to. I will come to visit you one of these days, when I am sure I can play the part.

They drew the curtains in the hospital and Daniel closed the shutters and returned to bed pulling the sheet above his face. Kalinsky woke up feeling a strong pain for the first time.

*   *   *

When Daniel was eighteen he was drafted. He had looked forward to it because being in uniform for him meant a change, equality with Yoram and adventures. The first few weeks distinguished him as a good soldier. He was eager to volunteer, to help, to obey. He had the discipline some of his mates lacked and an ability to operate alone at the same time. He volunteered as a paratrooper and the physical discomforts of being in this unit did not bother him. He coveted the silver wings and the red beret and somehow he even looked forward to the moment when he could send his father a picture of himself all decorated, an officer perhaps. The situation on the borders worsened and he had to stay in camp on week-ends as well, which turned Gilad into a remote memory composed of white shirts, hot water and good books.

When he jumped for the first time he experienced the usual fear, almost unexpectedly, and a few seconds later under the large dome of the parachute, an utter relaxation and a desire never to reach the approaching hard surface. He was afraid whenever he jumped, although his fear had nothing to do with the possibility of falling down with an unopened parachute. It was an illogical fear of the vacuum, of the speedy fall, of the lack of control knowing that the sensation which followed would be the happiest he had known. Special boots, new slang, the red hat on his head looking like an anemone in a wheat field, the graduation ceremony. Yoram and Rina were there, and it was then that he noticed for the first time that something was happening between them.

The silver wings were attached to his starched shirt, above the pocket. Yoram had them, many others had and deserved them, but these were his, and he touched the metal as if it was sacred. Haim Kalinsky, he thought, what do you know about jumping into empty space waiting to be jerked by the opening of the white canopy.

He wanted to be alone with Yoram the day he graduated but it was impossible with Rina around. Her own conscription was due soon and she was making plans for the three of them – secret missions, desert patrols, night raids, brilliant victories. They drove to Gilad together after the ceremony and on the way Yoram told him he was thinking of marrying Rina when she was through with the service.

When Rina was kissed and rejected by Daniel she knew he was unapproachable. After Daniel had gone into the army she met Yoram often, at first to ask about Daniel's progress and later for long walks gathering wild flowers and watching birds. She told Yoram Daniel did not want her, and when he held her hand once – crossing a stream – she sensed his strength and warmth and having crossed the stream left her hand in his. Yoram was shorter than Rina, but their two smiles could fill the world with glee and if she and Daniel had in common a certain sadness about some things, she shared with Yoram all that was bright and laughing. He kissed her on the harvest's stubble and behind hay stacks and he wove summer flowers in her curls and counted her freckles. Yoram loved with joy and innocence and she knew it was something to be grateful for though the first tremble of Daniel's touch never recurred and his gray melancholy still hovered above her when alone. She took to wearing dresses rather than shorts or slacks and though not curvy or buxom her body acquired a pleasant roundness where the thighs met the hips. Yoram decided to leave the service in a year unless war broke out and they would get married between Gilad and Shimron in their favourite spot under a eucalyptus tree.

Daniel was not made to feel lonely. He was happy about Rina and slightly jealous about Yoram, but once again he discovered the joy of being left out. He was alone without a need for a richer content and this did not bother him either. A few favourite poems drove away the budding worries as to his future, his deeper interests or desires or dreams.

He was made a full member of Gilad in a short, touching ceremony and small children on the lawn approached him, wanting to touch the new wings and try on the red beret. Kalinsky wrote an anxious letter. Were there not other things to do in the army, he wondered. After all he was an only son and the leftover of a great tragedy and perhaps he should be stationed in some HQ office. He was proud of him, too and there was something touching in the way he expressed his pride – Imagine, he wrote, a Kalinsky paratrooper, unbelievable! Your great-grandfather was a small merchant in Cracow and your ancestors were never closer to God than the height of a three-storey building. My son, high in the sky, alone, floating. He wanted to know who was responsible for folding the parachutes and now that he had his wings would it be necessary for him to do more jumps. Miriam was taking Hebrew lessons, determined to make it to Israel even if she had to go alone, and her pride was worth the fear and the discomfort. Daniel received a new watch from the Kibbutz secretary and his vacation was cut short by news of border tensions and the unit's mobilization.

Daniel discovered the ease with which he could kill. Not the joy, nor the hatred, nor the thought process of justifying the pressure on the trigger. Simply the thoughtless automatic obedience which resulted in a lifeless lump of a body somewhere in the dark. He was not a fierce soldier, but he was an excellent soldier. He loved his mates and he was quick during the night battles which were frequent then, and even when exhausted his senses were alert – detached from his mind and heart, animal-like and tense and quick. He had nobody to think about, he had no responsibilities, he was doing a job. In a few months he had a reputation as a reliable and courageous reconnaissance expert. He was especially fond of two boys in the small unit, a Yemenite and a Hungarian referred to as 'Black and White'. They were inseparable though utterly different in character and inclinations. During a raid across the lake one night they were both killed and for the first time in his life Daniel felt a sense of loss, of fear, of the proximity of death and the fact that survival was not to be taken for granted. When he was next involved in battle he shot to kill with a new sensation, crying as he released the grenades, ' For the Black and for the White, and once again for the Black . . . ' The enemy now was not an abstract idea, nor a historical obstacle in the way of complete national freedom. The enemy had to do with tomb-stones, with faces remembered alive and joking, with the sensation of shaking a strong hand which melts away suddenly and disappears leaving his own hand empty and turning it into a fist. The enemy now was the blackness where friends were sighing when wounded and the dawn light on stretchers when they were brought back. When his two friends were killed and the unit reassembled in the barracks, they spread their personal belongings on a camp bed and each of the living ones took some object of the dead. He had a pair of socks belonging to the White one, and they were clean and mended if not new. A friend was never left behind to be taken prisoner and Daniel was used to the weight of a human body, wounded and bleeding. The commander was a friend, the cook was a friend, ranks did not matter and the unit remained small and family-like, but even this clannish atmosphere could not soften the tension created by inevitable thoughts of – sooner or later it will be my turn. Courage surpassed the humanly possible, but then so did some of the tasks demanded of them and friendship could be, and frequently was, interrupted only by death.

Daniel was stationed in the south, as was Yoram, and later towards the spring of the following year Rina joined them. She looked good in her uniform and her sergeant's stripes gave an air of protectiveness rather than authority. Yoram was completing his service and Daniel was about to go to an officers' training school in spite of his resentment of the idea, but their few months together in Beer-Sheba were all dust-trails behind speeding jeeps, excursions to canyons and unexplored wadis and exposure of each of them to a landscape that stripped one of shadows, defences and mannerisms. They had their own slang and they needed fewer and fewer words to express what they felt. The bridge over the wadi was their meeting place. When Daniel was on a patrol or a raid Yoram and Rina waited at the bridge and he never failed to come, tired, covered with dust, at times scratched or lightly wounded, at times frustrated when nothing had happened.

'Why don't you find yourself a girl?' Yoram teased him often. 'Rina has a lot of friends, we could all go out then.'

'And offer her nights of tense waiting? Not yet.'

He never told them about Nechama. Nechama was not to be talked about and each of the men who knew her held the knowledge close to his own heart, it was understood that she was not to be discussed or mentioned. Each of a certain number of fighters had Nechama, alone, to himself, in a special way, not caring what and how she gave to others. That is why nobody told Daniel about Nechama, and she found him in the way she found the others. A moment of extreme fatigue at the end of a battle and insufficient sleep, a walk. She knew his name and she walked beside him suggesting they should have coffee at her place. He agreed, too tired to be either curious or cautious. She led the way to a second-floor flat over-crowded with furniture, pillows, stuffed animals and flowers.

'You know my name,' he said rather than asked.

'Yes. Black and White used to talk about you.'

He sank into a chair and watched her prepare the coffee

on a small kerosene lamp. She was in her thirties and handsome if not beautiful. Her skin was white and her hair black and long. She had green eyes and a large mouth and a mole on her chin. She took off her high-heeled shoes and he noticed how short she was.

'Don't you want to ask me what my name is?' she said. 'Nechama. The coffee will be ready in a few moments.'

His eyes felt heavy and his body comfortably relaxed and last night's battle sounds were beginning to fade away.

'Was Gideon badly wounded last night?' she asked.

'His arm,' he said.

He did not then, and never afterwards, ask her how she knew the names of the boys or their actions. Last night's was a secret raid but he accepted her knowledge of it and knew it to be safe. He sipped from the coffee cup and she massaged his back gently taking off his shirt.

'Come and lie down,' she said and he followed her to the bedroom. She undressed and he half-watched her do so, rather surprised at how fast all her clothes came off. She cuddled close to him and undressed him as if he were a baby.

'I'm exhausted,' he said. 'I've never been with a woman.'

'I know,' she smiled as her hand, soft, like tepid water, counted his ribs and pulled him to her. He made love to her, perspiring and clumsy, and she stroked his wet hair and whispered,

'Sleep now.'

When he woke up he was alone in the bed. There was nothing strange about his being there, he did not feel alone, the room looked familiar and its smell was of dying roses. She was fully dressed, her high heels elevating her

91

again and her mouth smeared with fresh lipstick.

'Another coffee,' she said, and walked out as he was dressing.

It was all very simple and very silent. He did not wonder about the unsaid or feel like exploring more.

'Do you have parents?' she asked.

'A father in Poland. I haven't seen him since the war. We correspond.'

When he mentioned Kalinsky he remembered that he had received and not answered three letters. He would write that night he decided.

'You're from a Kibbutz, aren't you?'

'Yes. Gilad.'

'You must know Yoram then,' she said.

'He's my closest friend.'

She asked him not to mention having met her to anybody, and he felt sure he wouldn't have done anyway and when he asked, 'May I come again?' he knew it was unnecessary to ask. When he left he took a mental note of the house and the street and wondered why he had not kissed her.

Nechama was not a prostitute. She was a woman who had lost her great love. He was a paratrooper and since his death she was 'their woman'. At times she worked as a waitress, a guide, a barmaid, but she followed the unit and they knew she was there and every night someone would come, for a minute or an hour or the whole night. When she was not alone she simply did not open the door, and if two friends met in the street in front of the house no questions were asked or cracks exchanged. Some talked to her about the dead friends she knew, some sat in silence or fell asleep, some laughed with her or made love or had a bath and a meal. She carried on her flesh the touch of fingers which were now feeding worms and she was the cleanest of women. To be with her meant to be with others who had died, with a spirit of destiny, of acceptance. For her, they were all fragments of the man she loved and his image was evoked every night anew, always, there with her in the laughter of Gideon or the dimples of Yoram, the shyness of Daniel or the fear, the anxiety, the premonitions, the tenderness and concern of the others.

The next raid was scheduled for a Saturday night and all leaves were cancelled. Daniel strolled along the lazy afternoon street and climbed the stairs. She opened the door and closed the shutters and he said, ' I forgot to kiss you last time.'

He kissed her and made love to her and she said, ' You are tired, take care tonight.'

Did she smell battles, he wondered, or approaching death? Did she sit there wondering who would not return? Was his effort to conceal the edginess he always felt before a raid betraying him?

He felt like never moving, lying there on his back. Her black hair wove a pattern on the pillow and her red mouth was slightly open. A knock was heard on the door. He jerked, clutching his battle-dress. She beckoned to him to return to bed and lay there silent. Another knock, footsteps descending the stairs and the echo of heavy boots on the asphalt road. For a brief moment he felt guilty. Then he wondered who the boy was and looking at his watch he realized it was time to leave. She kissed him with anxiety in her eyes. To say to Nechama, ' I hope to see you again,' was not a figure of speech. It meant, ' I hope to survive this one too, I hope to be alive tomorrow.' When he walked up the road he heard footsteps behind him, the heavy boots again, and he never turned to look who it was seeking a moment of reassurance in the lap of a woman who lived with death. The kind of death they knew.

*   *   *

Daniel never mentioned Nechama and he never thought of other women either. A few girls tried to get close to him, but gave up when he seemed to remain indifferent. He was used to Rina, but on the whole the sight of girls in uniform did not please him. He never gave a thought to Nechama when fighting, but on the way to the frontier, when crowded in jeeps or command cars, the boys grew silent as if contemplating their chances, her figure floated among them like a cold caress. And with dawn's chill on the way back, many of them carried her image along the straight, monotonous road. Daniel would examine their faces, many were asleep or pretending to be, and reflected in their eyes was Nechama, the lover, the comforter, the woman, the witch, a good luck charm, the evil eye. He would then close his eyes too, and sail away to the stale roses and white sheets.

Yoram left the army and returned to Gilad, returning south for reserve service often enough, and Rina was transferred to the Jerusalem Command where she enrolled in the University and began to study Archaeology. Daniel spent a year in courses and was a company commander at twenty and Kalinsky continued to write letters, seldom answered. The distance grew between Poland and Daniel. It was immense when he was in Gilad and now the smell of smoke and dynamite and the yellow stretches of the desert enlarged it. He wrote his father not to worry, he was doing well and had a safe job in the army. With the consent of the Kibbutz he decided to prolong his service, and he made it to Gilad only on week-ends to drink thirstily the greens and the browns and the laughter of children swimming in the river. Now Yoram waited for him and Daniel enjoyed recounting stories. They resumed their long afternoon walks, but Yoram's nights belonged to Rina.

Kalinsky wrote that business was bad and he had applied for an exit visa. ' It is a question of time and patience now that the decision has been taken,' he wrote. ' Once we get our visas we shall pack and leave and we can reunite at last my son.' ' Perhaps,' he added, ' we could start some business together in one of the new cities where Miriam can attend high-school.' Daniel dismissed the thought as unreal and automatically answered to say how happy he would be when they were able to come.

There were rumours of an approaching war in the air and the soldiers were restless. The general mobilization included Yoram, and Daniel was given twelve-hour leave. In Gilad there was talk of a large-scale attack on Jordan, and Rina stayed the night.

' I shall come along too,' she declared. ' There is nothing to do in the unit I am with '

She was nervous and irritable and when the men prepared to leave there were tears in her eyes. Daniel excused himself and walked out of the room pretending he had forgotten something and when he returned Rina was gone and Yoram was sitting in the car serious and pensive.

' Anything wrong?'

' No, she thinks we're not capable of taking care of ourselves. That's all. She said to tell you to take care.'

They drove to Tel-Aviv and to the Southern Command where they had to part. Daniel had to join his company and Yoram was with another.

' Do you know what it's all about?'

' Not really, I suppose we'll jump, tonight, somewhere, and if you're attached to the artillery we may meet on the ground. I'll look for you anyway.'

' We may meet before, in Beer-Sheba. If there's a delay I'll be there, tonight, at Morris's.'

' Or after the battle, on the bridge, as usual.'

They shook hands and Daniel drove off, turning to look at Yoram who was wearing an old battle-dress and carrying a small haversack. The last few years had left a mark on Yoram's face. He had the same smiling eyes, but in the corners was a flicker of seriousness, a sense of responsibility and tenderness. They were going to get married in the spring, Rina would work as an archaeologist in the North and Yoram would continue working in the fish ponds of Gilad. ' Many children, five or six perhaps,' they said.

It was late fall, a low gray ceiling of sky, static and metallic. There was no movement in the air and the first flowers of autumn dotted the fields pink and yellow. Daniel made it to his camp on time and the officers' dining room returned him to the atmosphere of excitement, guesses, preparations.

The Sinai was the target. He had twenty-four hours to prepare his unit and he felt relieved. The Sinai. He had crossed the frontier before, many times, but somehow it felt different. He was amused at the thought of sending his father photographs of his son near Mount Sinai. The commotion in the barracks was contagious. During the last few weeks, the soldiers were held back, in spite of steady infiltration from Egypt which resulted in the deaths of women and children and loss of property. Eve of battle. Some were writing letters, cracking jokes to release tension, a song in a corner, a check-up of the weapons and equipment, guesses, plans. Daniel made sure all was in order and took the road to Beer-Sheba wondering whether Yoram would be there. At dawn they had to board the planes. When the lights of his jeep spilled into the main street it was close to midnight. The streets were empty but the restaurant crowded and Yoram wasn't there. Daniel had a steak and walked to Nechama's street. It was a cold night and he thought of her small gas stove and coffee. There was no light in the window but he went up and knocked on the door. She let him in, into the dark room and embraced him. Suddenly she was not the woman he knew. She was a frightened girl seeking protection and he stroked her hair and bare arms.

'What is it? Why don't we put on some lights?'

'Please, no, it's better this way.'

He touched her face and his fingertips felt the warm wetness of tears. He asked no more. They sat in the dark, she was leaning against him counting and recounting his long fingers.

'Did you ever play the piano?'

'No. My brother did, Shmuel.'

'Where is he now?'

'I think he was killed in the war. The world war.'

'Yes, I keep forgetting you are from Poland,' she said. 'Daniel,' she whispered softly, 'could we lie in bed without making love? Just hold me in your arms, and leave when you have to.'

'You don't want to tell me why you're crying?'

She did not answer and began to undress in the dark.

It was a windy night and whirlpools of sand hit the pavement and the walls like blind bats. She relaxed in his arms and when he thought she was asleep he gently covered her and dressed to go. When the guard in camp saluted him and he drove to his room he noticed he had forgotten his watch at Nechama's. Something to go back for, he thought, and made the best of three hours of sleep left him.

When Yoram went to see Nechama there was a light in her window. He was in a good mood and he knocked on the door announcing himself. It was past three in the morning, but Nechama was all dressed up as if ready to go out. She was not surprised to see him and, unable to resist the laughter in his eyes, asked him in smiling.

' I think I'll never see you again. I'm getting married soon and unless you come up North there isn't much chance of my coming by.'

' Unless there are more wars,' she laughed.

' I'm not a baby any more. I've had my share of dust. I am going to father half a dozen babies, lose my hair slowly, develop a belly and feed fish.'

' Not a bad life. Are you off tonight?'

' Tomorrow.'

He noticed Daniel's watch and took hold of it.

' Daniel?' he asked.

She nodded.

' May I keep it? I'll see him somewhere one of these days, he'll need it and we're friendly enough not to ask too many questions.'

She shrugged and he put the watch on his wrist.

' You lose the touch,' he said, ' or so it seems, and I feel strange in uniform now. It seems less important, less meaningful and I know the young ones are better than I

98

could ever be.'

' You've had your share.'

' I suppose it's just talk. Once I'm at it again I'll feel at home, only that none of us are real soldiers, we need a reason to fight, a motivation and an urge.'

' Don't you have it? '

' Of course, but with the years the reasons not to fight accumulate too. Now it's Rina. Later – the children, the farm. It started when I felt responsible for Daniel, before he found his father.'

' Of all the boys I know,' she said, ' he resembles most the one I lost.'

' You lost many, Nechama.'

' I lost one. The others were a repetition of the same pain.'

' Well, perhaps this is a last battle for all of us.'

' Would you mind terribly if I ask you to leave? ' she asked.

' Of course not. I just came to say good-bye in case I go straight to Gilad when this one is over. There's a red-head waiting for me and she's a worrying type! '

He kissed her forehead and left.

Chapter Six

The sound of propellers was like the overture to an opera, and the night landscape framed in the opening of the Nord aircraft was familiar. Daniel was still sleepy but the morning chill and the tight parachute straps helped to wake him completely. The lights underneath disappeared as they crossed the border and he checked his personal equipment for maps, compass, some tinned food and first-aid kit. The desert below was lunar and dead and the jokes in the aircraft had to do with Moses' exodus, forty years in the desert and the golden calf. Peaks of mountains could be discerned and an occasional light flickered with enmity. They timed the trip and were descending now to the marked area. Warning light, last few words and the brief silence before the actual jump, a blast of cold wind carried him sideways and tossed him around. For a short moment he felt he was going upwards, towards the stars and the Milky Way, and he straightened himself as the parachute spread and stabilized him. His eyes were accustomed to the darkness and the pale gray of dawn could be seen painting the horizon with a thin brush. Down below the night was still black and sheltering and when he approached the ground he could see a few of the boys folding their parachutes. He was ready in a few moments and, in spite of an hour of confusion, by dawn the company was well camouflaged between two hills and guarding the hilltops as well. There was nothing to do for a while but wait for orders. Infantry and artillery columns were to join them from the East and the North and they were not to move in the area unless an enemy force revealed itself to be inferior in numbers. He dozed off, watching a lizard on a rock, and occasionally sipped some tinned orange juice – what they called ' heart-burn juice '.

When finally the company was sent to patrol the canyon, pandemonium broke out. Daniel and his men were ordered to follow in to rescue them and blood touched blood. Once again he was not thinking, once again jealous hatred was evoked by the sight of the dead and automatically he released hand grenades into the caves and followed in with the machine-gun's scathing fire. He was scratched in his arm and thigh and lost some blood but all that mattered were the black jaws of the enemy-held caves dug into the steep slopes and the badly injured friends on the hillside, losing their holds and rolling down into the valley like useless bundles. The moaning of the wounded hurt him physically and when, with a sudden deafening silence, the battle was over, he carried someone a long way away before he realized he was burdened with an enemy soldier. Blood was spilling from an enormous wound, and Daniel knew he was not going to last the long descent. He propped his head against a rock, disarmed him and hurried back to join the others.

There was no time to share the distress of having paid too dear a price for a victory or the counting of the dead and wounded. Orders were received and he was to take off with a small platoon to meet an approaching column and direct them back to the canyon. When he returned with the platoon after completing his mission he saw the Northern column advancing, and in one of the first armed trucks Yoram's round face could be seen. They embraced and Yoram knew better than to ask questions. Daniel's face was gray and fallen and they drove silently to the small camp in the hills.

Black satin of night engulfed the human débris and hid the blood, the amputated limbs and the mangled bodies. Night covered tears in the eyes of the older soldiers and revengeful anger in the eyes of the young boys and when Daniel fell asleep Yoram remembered the child he had rescued and the long trip from Bari on an unseaworthy Greek boat. The night was cold and blankets taken out and if someone hummed a song it was not a happy one. There was no moon in the sky, a complete blackness was on the hills and spoken words sounded false and out of place. The vehicles were covered with mud and looked like the harmless toys of a giant's children.

Two hours after midnight the captain suggested a reconnaissance patrol to the bridge over the wadi. If the bridge was not guarded or mined they might cross it and check the condition of the road to the canal. Daniel was about to leave with two other soldiers when Yoram stopped him.

' Where to? ' Yoram asked.

' Oh, just a morning walk around the hills. Do you want to come along? '

' Sure.'

Yoram jumped up and again they were walking like they did along the banks of the Jordan, but in the middle of the Sinai. The two soldiers behind were armed and suspicious and when they reached a plateau from which they could see the road and the wadi Daniel ordered them to keep cover and he advanced with Yoram towards the silhouette of the bridge. The pebbles in the wadi shone white and the road was black and covered with wandering dunes. They were under the bridge now and couldn't see any signs of life. Daniel said:

' Wait here and I'll go up and check. If there's a guard he's either asleep or single. Otherwise we would have heard some conversation.'

Yoram grabbed his arm.

' Please, I'll do it. Good for my morale. I've been riding a jeep until now as if going to a wedding. It'll only take a few minutes and I'll be back.'

He looked at his watch and remembered it was Daniel's, but crawled away holding on to his submachine-gun.

Daniel did not mind. Many times he had felt like doing something instead of a friend and since Yoram was his senior, he couldn't very well tell him to obey orders. There was no danger in the air, it was a clear night and a bright polar star was taking ursa minor for a night stroll. He was absorbed in his thoughts when he heard Yoram's voice.

' It looks deserted all right, what now? '

' We'll go back and they'll send someone with a mine detector. Let's go.'

What followed took only a few seconds. Yoram walked several steps along the bridge meaning to jump down to where Daniel was. Then an explosion, footsteps of the soldiers running towards them and the sight of Yoram holding his belly and moaning. Daniel bent to him pale and unbelieving.

' It was a mine,' he said and tried to find the wound.

Both his legs were crushed and the rest of his body was

covered with blood. With two guns and battle-dresses they improvised a stretcher and began the long walk back.

' Mother,' Yoram groaned.

' You'll be all right,' Daniel said automatically, still in a state of shock.

' You never know,' Yoram said.

' Don't talk, we'll be at the camp soon.'

Yoram was sighing and his body felt heavier and heavier as the crust of the desert gave way and their heavy boots sank into it. Suddenly he cried out. He was in uncontrollable pain and Daniel told the boys to lower the stretcher and bring the medic over. He was left alone with Yoram and he could say nothing.

' I should never have let you go.'

Yoram opened his eyes. They held the usual smile, and he was trying to say something amusing, as always. He searched for Daniel's hand and held it tight, folding it up in pain.

' Water,' he said.

' Not yet.' Daniel had to refuse, suspecting stomach wounds.

' My legs,' he sighed.

' It will be all right.'

Yoram's face was cruelly lit by the dawn. It was gray and distorted. From the waist down Daniel could see nothing but blood and bone and flesh. The medic arrived with a few soldiers.

' What's he doing here? ' he asked, pointing to Yoram and bending down to tend to him.

' He came along with me, it was a mine.'

' He's not from your unit.'

' He's a reserve soldier. We thought we would do it together.'

104

The medic began muttering, and when the white bandages soaked immediately with blood he looked up again at Daniel.

'He has to be taken away. He should be operated on so we'd better order a helicopter.'

'He's not going to die.' Daniel grabbed the medic by the arm.

'Not if his stomach is put together again. There's nothing more we can do here.'

'He can't die!' Daniel screamed.

Two soldiers took Yoram, who was now unconscious, away on a stretcher and Daniel was left behind, unable to move. Somewhere between his gullet and his stomach emptiness settled and his hands were frozen. The blood was drained from his veins and when the medic returned he found him still standing there gazing vaguely ahead.

'Come on, I'll give you an injection. Is it the first time you've seen blood?'

'It was my fault. I should never have let him go. I don't need an injection and I've seen more dead friends than anybody would want to have in a lifetime.'

He began to regain his composure, and started walking towards the camp.

'Where is he?'

'He was taken away. They will drive him on to the next camp where there are some other injured soldiers already waiting in a helicopter. He should be operated on in a few hours in Beer-Sheba and you'll see him when you get back. The captain asked to see you.'

He told the captain the story and received the conventional comforting speech – 'It happens to all of us, he'll be all right.' Daniel asked to be sent back as soon as possible.

'It depends on our next mission. If I don't need you I'll treat it as a special case but don't forget we're in the middle of a war.'

It meant nothing now. He was used to night-raids which terminated with sunrise, and now war was a long wait. War was dirty socks and the supply-car being late, the itching stubble on his face and the sound of aeroplanes occasionally. War became a list of people lost in the canyon and the gouts of Yoram's blood this arid soil had swallowed. A few enemy officers were taken prisoners, they were pathetic and yielding and he had no hatred for them. He wondered whether Yoram's mother knew he was injured, and Rina, and how he could face any of them. He felt he had to go back and again ask to be transferred. Two days later most of the peninsula was in Israeli hands and civilians could be seen taking sight-seeing tours of the desert their ancestors took forty years to cross. Daniel left for Beer-Sheba by plane and he was allowed to do so not because of his rank but because it seemed useless to keep him there guarding Egyptian prisoners and waiting for orders. When he got to the hospital he did not have to ask for Yoram. In the corridor like the chorus of tragedy sat his parents and Rina, who burst into tears when she saw him.

' He asked for you,' said the father.

' Can I see him? '

' Not now. He was worse tonight and they're operating again.'

Rina couldn't talk and when they crossed the road to the café and were alone she said :

' Tell me what happened.'

Daniel did and she begged him not to tell the parents.

' Say he was sent with you and there was a mine on the

bridge. There's no need to take the blame or present it as a childish useless accident.'

' What do the doctors say? Is he going to recover? '

' They amputated both legs,' she said and was crying now.

The redness of her eyes matched her face and her hair.

' He lost a lot of blood and there were complications.'

In the waiting room in front of the stove Yoram's mother was holding a handkerchief. In it were her son's personal belongings and Daniel's watch was still counting the seconds. All Kibbutz watches were the same, he thought, knowing this to be his, they wouldn't be able to tell. Yoram's mother was a brave woman and a hard-working one and she stared at Daniel with a demanding look. Was she thinking that motherless boys ought to take priority in death, so there is less hurt in the world?

' I'll be back,' he said and motioned to Rina not to follow him.

When Nechama opened the door she was startled. Only after he washed up he realized what he had looked like, but didn't care. She didn't know about Yoram and when he told her, her eyes were hard, almost cruel, as if a presentiment of hers had come true.

' What a way to die,' she said.

' He's not dead! ' He grabbed her and hurt her arm and let go.

' I'm sorry. There isn't a good way and a bad way to die and there's no need to talk like that.'

' He took your watch,' she said, softer now.

' I know, his mother has it.'

' We've won the war. There will be peace now.'

' Until the next one.'

A terrible suspicion crossed his mind. He thought she

107

waited for death and fed on it. He thought he heard regret in her voice when she mentioned *peace* as if everything that made her exist would disappear suddenly. He got up to leave.

' Don't,' she said.

' I have to go back to the hospital. I have to talk to him.'

He pushed her away and he ran, breathing heavily, until he reached the hospital entrance.

' Not yet,' Rina said. ' They need some blood, we gave some to the blood bank.'

Daniel went to the first floor and gave his name and rank, and blood type.

He lay on a hard bed and his arm was smeared with alcohol, before the needle pierced the skin and settled in the blood stream. The glass jar hanging above him was filling up at a maddeningly slow pace and he could not feel the needle any more.

Did he ever pray? Was he praying now? He wanted the blood to continue dripping into the glass container, more and more of it, and be injected into Yoram's arteries. He wanted his own legs to be amputated and grafted to Yoram's chopped thighs so he could walk with Rina on the road from Gilad to Shimron and play with the children. He did not notice his tears but when the nurse came to check the needle she wiped his eyes. She pulled the needle out and took his blood away, saying without turning:

' Please don't get up yet, you can rest where you are for a few minutes.'

He closed his eyes and once again they were under the bridge.

' Careful with the pebbles,' Yoram told him, and it

was all so simple, like deciding who would have a shower first in the Kibbutz shower-room.

He remembered there was no tension or dangerous silence. Yoram wanted to climb up and check the bridge and he let him go and then he heard the explosion – did he ever stop hearing the explosion? – and now Yoram had stubs instead of legs and a pulp of intestines instead of a stomach and his mother was downstairs waiting for news. He opened his eyes and noticed his own legs – long and healthy and suddenly fatigue took over and he felt the bed swaying like the waves under the ship in Bari. When he opened his eyes he felt nausea and Rina's freckled hand was on his arm.

This was ten years ago and he wondered now which room he had been in, and whether there was a window? It didn't matter really though, since he had learned to shed sentimental memories. A street corner, a dry flower in a box, old letters and even photographs, all were dismissed and forgotten. Memories of a tune or a voice, old clothes, unit emblems were all folded and put away, with the yesterdays and the tomorrows. Suppose Isaac had had to sacrifice his father, would it have held as much meaning, he wondered and pulled the chair to the window.

* * *

Kalinsky was in pain. He had experienced pain before, but this was different. Somehow it did not contain the promise of an eventual climax and then the letting go. Like an odious obtrusive guest it was there to stay, he felt, with its dull sensation of pressure. He had to accommodate it somehow and it felt like a permanent addition to his bodily sensations. From now on, he knew, there would be fatigue, and hunger at times, and the need for natural relief and this pain. He asked the nurse to push the bed to the window and prop him up. Across the road in the distance were the dune hills. He hated the desert sand and the dust. He hated taking off his shoes and socks to find that grains of sand had settled between his toes. There was dust in Dora's hair and grains of sand on her body and he longed for smooth surfaces. Why did someone tell him he would like the desert? He did not find it majestic or imposing or pure or spacious. He felt trapped in its space and the monotony of yellow bored him. It mocked his tight collars and soft skin. Between his window and the dunes the city stretched under-developed fingers in all directions. Each row of houses simply disappeared where the sands took over and a few trees could be seen struggling beyond them. The buildings looked small and insignificant and although the city was growing it seemed to shrink whenever the southerly wind brought gifts of dust to cover the asphalt, the pavements and the car tracks. The city could never become home, he knew, but he was tied to it by ropes of wind and yellow chilling grains meaninglessly and uselessly.

In the corner of his window, between himself and the city, the sun laughed. It was an alien sun. The sun he liked was the one which appeared at the end of a cold winter, friendly, welcome, kindly, melting the snows and throwing gentle light on the pear trees in the garden. He knew the sun one could bask in, without the need to protect oneself, without fear, on his own terms. This one was a red devil. This sun was his enemy from the first day and he was doomed to renew the exhausting battle daily knowing that sunset was not really his own victory. He woke up every morning with this enemy above him and all day long the battle continued. Every evening Kalinsky experienced a rebirth, but by then he was fatigued and drained out and needed his few hours of sleep to be able to face the satanic beams of sunrise.

He looked down to the street. He saw Lipsky in the café and for a second he wished Lipsky's café was on the second floor. He could talk to him across the road. He liked Lipsky from a distance, he was even curious about Lipsky. They shared the secret knowledge of things as they should be – real wide streets, a real river, city traffic and rush hours. They conversed in Yiddish and although it was never stated in so many words, they both wanted to be sitting once again in a smoky café in Warsaw or in Bucharest, being nobodies in a comfortable way and enjoying the familiar routine of a dash of fear, a tinge of suspicion, anonymity, avoidance of exposure and, at times, limited success in some small-scale business. A few Bedouins were squatting in front of the hospital. His feelings about them ranged from distrust and suspicion to indifference. Miriam told him they were hospitable and loyal but all he could see were black robes and thick dark skin, a foreign language and strange customs. He did not feel superior, but they were simply not his equals.

Daniel was south, Miriam had said, but it was impossible to look south from his window and the pain in his chest was soaring. He called the nurse. He liked ringing for the nurse. When the pain was not so strong he almost waited for it to reach a pitch which would justify ringing for the nurse. Whenever one of the three other patients in the room was attended by the nurse he always watched carefully trying to convince himself that they were not treated with the same attention and warmth as he

111

was. He had to exhaust all the privileges of the very ill. He enjoyed complaining about the food. He waited every day at eleven for the young nurse to come and change his bed sheets and pyjamas and he felt his body for new aches wishing the doctors would stay longer near his bed on their daily round. He also knew he was going to die. So what mattered now was not the great issues of life and death but the stale taste of cold mashed potatoes. He was not preoccupied with summing up his life or wondering about the next world but with the snoring of the other patients and the thinness of the bath towels. Defying death had to do with a ripe and juicy apple and the softness of the mattress. Self-pity dared not touch the growth in his lungs and concentrated fully and stubbornly on a cut on his cheek while shaving, a back-ache he developed from lying in bed without moving and the fact that Dora was leaving earlier than the other visitors.

The nurse came in, patient and smiling. She was Yemenite and her skin was dark. Kalinsky felt sorry for the dark-skinned Jews and there, in Beer-Sheba, he was slightly envious of them as they were at home, he thought. But then Beer-Sheba should be populated by the dark-skinned and he should have been given a house in the north, in a large city, the kind he was used to. They never had it better, he thought, and they should be grateful, but at his age he deserved an easier life. The nurse's name was Rachel and she pronounced it with a Yemenite accent which lent it an exotic and special touch. He always thought that dark skin must be coarse and unpleasant to touch and was rather surprised when she placed her hand on his forehead to find it smooth and feminine. She gave him some bitter yellow medicine which he swallowed in one gulp and promised to check again later. There was

112

something insolent about her happy smile. It was not a professional smile and it had hope, and he knew she knew he was dying and how could she bear to smile.

Dora did not smile. Dora arrived every day after five and pulled the oil-painted wooden chair from under the bed. It was an uncomfortable chair and her bulky thighs spilled over it. Every day after five she sat on it with a sigh and placed her handbag on the floor. *Nu,* Haim, she said and he proceeded to tell her what he had been doing during the day. She listened carefully, very seldom interrupting for more details. If he said, ' the nurse said ', she would ask ' Rachel? ' and add ' a good girl ', at times repeating the sentence. Haim told her about his pains, the small pains of discomfort. He did not tell her about the big pain. He told her about his small thoughts and often asked her to come nearer to him and whispered something in her ear about one of the other patients. When he was through, and there was not much to tell she would pull out of her hand a paper bag with something for him: fruit or chocolates which he did not touch, a piece of cake or a strudel. He smiled faintly, thanking her, and asked for news and she would say, ' the same ', at times adding a few words about the shop she now ran on her own or about Miriam and Shmuel. Miriam was pregnant and was not feeling well and when she could come and visit she did, but the smell of the ward and the sight of her sick father made her feel worse and Haim understood it. Dora brought him the Polish newspaper every day and he never looked at it while she was still there, as much as he wanted to.

Then there was silence, without drama or tension or fear of words. Dora looked through the window and Haim stared at the ceiling and the evening settled in like gray flakes of cotton wool, first at the corners, padding them out softly, then spreading along the walls and the washed tiles until it was necessary to switch on the light. Whenever this happened, although she did not have to, Dora stood up and straightened her wrinkled summer dress, picked up her handbag and said first to Haim ' Well, I think I shall go now ', and he nodded and then she wished the other patients good night and walked out, always turning to look back at him when she reached the door, always smiling when she did. Her last smile crawled towards him and comforted him in a special way until the following day.

When Dora left Haim read the newspaper with the interest and intensity of someone who is responsible for what is written in it. When he disagreed he was angry in the manner of someone who was in a position to correct the error and cause matters to be handled differently immediately. When he read of a political move which pleased him he nodded sagely in consent and pride. He was impatient and his disagreement was usually expressed in mumbling something like ' well, what can you expect? ' and developing his own suggestions. He was sure he knew how to avoid the prospect of inflation, how to achieve peace with the Arabs, how to handle the refugee problem or cope with a drought. He was lying in bed on the second floor every evening being a general and a prime minister, a cabinet member and an economic adviser, the president of other countries – Russia and America alternately displeased him – and an expert in all fields. When dinner was served he was still involved with what he had read and it was then that he condescended to talk to the other patients while breaking the soft boiled egg and sipping the soup. In the middle of dinner and conversation today he felt a new pain. It was not any sharper than the usual dull

114

pain but it was more definite and for a second he thought he could not breathe. Involuntarily he moaned and someone must have rung for the nurse because she was there with an injection ready. His tray was removed and a white partition was placed between his bed and the others. The drug relaxed him and he closed his eyes. 'The doctor will be in later,' the night nurse told him, and he was grateful for the isolating partition which enabled him to be alone with Daniel.

Daniel never left his mind. Sometimes it was only his face and eyes, at other times he could hear his voice and physically sense his nearness. When he drifted away it was never to disappear entirely but rather to cringe on the periphery of his mind where logic slows down and fantasy takes over. Daniel was there in the heat of the day in the little shop, he was to be seen in his grandson Shmuel's naughtiness and in jeeps and trucks loaded with soldiers or young men roaming the city. Never far, always ungraspable, Daniel was all the things Kalinsky wasn't, and none of the things he wanted him to be, and even if at moments the parallels neared and warmed each other, they never really touched.

To his left now, as he was lying on his back, was the white cloth stretched taut on white wooden frames and to his right the white curtain thin enough to let the moonlight through. Shrouded, he thought, as Daniel's image approached from above. There were so many things to say to him. Some were simple, about Dora and Miriam – was he never going to see them afterwards, afterwards being now the word he used instead of death? Also a strange desire: he wanted to be buried in the cemetery at Gilad. It was foreign and far and the soil was not his but he knew Daniel could not refuse such a simple wish, he would tell him when he saw him. He had to tell him that he did not regret coming to Israel. He did not love it, or hate it, nor had he tried hard enough to fit in or break away. He never quite understood why he should have come, and once he had come he resented being reduced in size. But he did not resent the country, he wanted to tell his son. He had to warn his son too, he had to tell him about an old man he knew in Warsaw. The man was a just man, a saint. He was a sage and a fountain of wisdom and knowledge and he evoked the same in others. He, Kalinsky, did not visit him very often but whenever he did he left with renewed faith and a purer mind. Although the man knew the secrets of the Kabbala he was a simple man, a teacher. He had gone off to Israel some time after Haim, and Haim saw him again in Jerusalem a few years later. The man had dried up. He was still a teacher but something had been lost, the man had stopped dreaming. He was still doing and learning and teaching and was still admired and respected but something was fading away, the mystery was gone, the journey had ended, and Haim regretted having seen him in Jerusalem the way he did. He had to warn Daniel, to tell him.

Would Daniel learn to say Kaddish, he wondered, a boy who had never prayed? He remembered him in synagogues on Yom Kippur as a child. He was going to fast, and did until noon, and then he asked for water and had his food. He remembered him asking the four questions on Passover with a thin monotonous voice concentrating on remembering the words and blushing whenever he had to be helped by Shmuel. Of course he would say Kaddish, he comforted himself, remembering again the shock he had when Daniel told him he was never Bar-Mitzvahed in Gilad. Yet, all this did not really matter, and the way to God, he knew,

116

was not blocked by bearded men and the square letters in the prayer book. There were other things he had to tell him. Was he really unable to come? Perhaps they had lied to him, perhaps he was not south but north enjoying the coolness of the Jordan water and working in the cowshed? Perhaps he was in Tel-Aviv gay and busy or right here, around the corner, across the road?

He felt no pain now, only sweet weakness. He would have liked to feel Daniel's strong hand on his shoulder, on his brow, on his balding head. Daniel never touched him. He touched his own body, gently as if bidding it farewell. There were the hairy hands – the tattooed number, the scar on the right arm. His ribs were showing and his hands slid along them like a stick along a ladder to the groin. His testicles felt like useless empty organs and he did not touch them. He placed his hands on his chest, where the pain was and undisturbed by the snores of the other patients, the distant drone of an aeroplane and footsteps in the corridor he sank into drugged sleep.

Was his father expecting him, Daniel wondered, and in what manner? Was he supposed to sit vigilant and quiet at his bedside and watch him give way? Were they expected to indulge in little stories and conversations in order not to *think*? There was nothing he could do to help and he was thinking of leaving town. He would visit his father and tell him he had to leave and go back. Anywhere. The room grew smaller with the hours and even the emptiness of the other room wasn't soothing any more. It could happen any day, but suppose it did not. Perhaps he had the strength to fight it off, or the will, or the faith, and he could neither die nor recover. He could not stand there day after day watching the window across the road, lacking the will to cross it or the courage to leave. He could go south for a few days, join Rina in Shivta maybe and return for the week-end. He could talk to Miriam and the doctor and find out more, find out everything.

Chapter Seven

What did they do with Yoram's legs? Did they burn them with the blood that stained the bandages? He gave Yoram blood and he woke up to find Rina there and they went for a wordless walk. When they returned Yoram's parents were not to be seen in the waiting room and a solemn nurse said the doctor had asked to talk to them. Where did Rina's tears come from? They just streamed down her cheeks but her face did not move and her eyes remained wide open. She wept silently, detached from her own tears, almost unaware of them. When Yoram's parents returned to the room they took their seats on the bench again – old and proud. They did not look grave or dramatic, their faces held the childish innocence of incredibility. Daniel and Rina looked at them and did not dare ask and they looked back and there was no need to ask. Certainty hung between them and none dared grasp it and shake it.

The doctor returned to them and said:

'You may come in now. He is still unconscious but there is nothing we can do. Perhaps you would like to be alone with him.'

Yoram's bed was the only one in the little room – did they give him a private room from the beginning or did they move him in as the privilege of the dying, Daniel wondered now. He remembered the sensation of entering the room. The four of them stopped on the narrow threshold and indulged in the ritual politeness of letting each other pass first. Each wanted to be alone with Yoram, but each needed the other's presence, as Yoram was not really there. He was bandaged and two sheets hiding a blanket covered the emptiness of the lower part of his body. His face was unscratched though slightly swollen, and it was perhaps the first time that Daniel had seen him completely smileless, mature and serious, as if matching the finality of the occasion.

There was only one chair in the room and Yoram's mother sat on it, Rina behind her holding her shoulders gently. The two men stood near the window with their backs to the living winter street. How long they stood there, Daniel would never know. Perhaps all four seasons brushed against the white walls with winter's greens and autumn's pink flowers and spring's golden wheat and summer's mauve bare mountains. Maybe it was all the hours they had had with the young man lying there, or all the hours they would never have or just one long pause, breathless and choking. The doctor came in and went away and a nurse brought a chair for the older man and they never looked at each other but looked at their child, her man, his friend, as if intense vigil could restore life or quicken the weakening pulse or revive the movement of blood and juices and muscles.

The sun sets early in Beer-Sheba in November and as Yoram's face grew darker the nurse came in again to adjust the infusion bottle which looked like a useless toy, independent of the veins it fed. She put on the light which made them shiver and left again as if ashamed. Daniel felt Rina's hand on his arm and jerked. She pulled him away

120

to the corridor.

'Let them be alone with him,' she said, but he did not hear, or reply or really care.

They sat on a bench in the corridor and suddenly they both knew it was all over. Rina grasped his hand in hers and the soft sound of crying reached them from the room.

'I let him die,' Daniel said.

Suddenly Rina next to him was a woman, never to be a girl again.

'Don't ever say that again,' she said, and he noticed her eyes were dry and her mouth hard.

The doctor came dressed in uniform and opened the door. The two old people were embracing each other facing the dead Yoram and the old man's tears were mercilessly illuminated by the light. Daniel stood up and looked at them and turned to go.

'I will come to Gilad,' he said to Rina, and he walked away along the corridor down the stairs, crossing the courtyard through the entrance gate into the street. It was raining lightly and he thanked each drop which joined his tears until he reached the centre of town and head-quarters. A supply truck was being loaded and he found room on it and the roar of the engine drowned his sobs as he returned to the unit.

The war was over, victory won and there was nothing for him to do. They would bury Yoram in Gilad, and he could feel the black mud heavy with rain water closing in on him. The rain made grave-digging difficult and when the area was cleared and the black toothless jaw opened it filled with water during the night.

The cemetery at Gilad was on the slope of a hill over-looking the valley, so it could not be seen from below. The gravestones were flat and small and each name was

121

charged with living images for those who visited the hill. There was no need to describe the dead or list their qualifications. A name, an age, the date of death. The war dead stayed together, in a straight military line as if still marching in formation somewhere. There were thirteen of them.

Daniel arrived early and climbed the hill, bypassing the village. The clouds played a game with the sun, which kept finding loopholes through which to shine on raindrops gathered on the leaves of wild irises. His boots were heavy with mud and he spread his wind-cheater jacket on a tombstone. He was weary. He felt he had been walking for months. He remembered the excitement of war, the dreary disappointment of war, the price to pay, the sterile corridors, the prisoners' sheds, Mount Sinai beautiful and meaningless to him, the traces of tears on Rina's cheeks, the traces of jets in the sky and the bare feet of enemy deserters breaking the surface of the dunes. He held his head in his hands, covering his frozen ears, and shut his eyes. What was tiring was not the road already travelled but the absence of a road ahead. He made up his mind about the unit. He would quit as soon as he could. Coward, he thought, don't you want to avenge Yoram, and opened his eyes to stare at the soft grass that grew gently embracing the yellow marble stones. He would leave the army, there was nothing he could do there, and wait for his father to come. He would help him settle down, teach him Hebrew, find him a job, give him a country. When he thought of this Yoram was suddenly there, smiling again for the first time since they covered his face with a white sheet.

When Daniel woke up the sky was clogged with low hanging clouds. The valley lay dormant in dull bland colours and the asphalt roads looked like fresh whip scars across its back. The funeral procession was approaching the hill and Daniel continued to sit on the stone watching them. The people of Gilad did not have black mourning clothes, and only black scarves could be seen here and there. The few cars and tractors stopped at the narrow path and a few paratroopers lifted the coffin to carry it. No sobbing was heard, footsteps sank in the wet grass without an echo and there was no wind in the air. He got up and stretched his stiff limbs. Now he could see the bearded army rabbi and Rina's face. He could see Yoram's parents and feel the weight of the coffin. For a moment he wanted to run away, then to snatch the coffin single-handed and carry his friend, his brother, his beloved alone, somewhere else. Then he put his beret on and waited for them to approach, avoiding their eyes, avoiding his own heartbeats.

The silent body of people moved among the graves. Occasionally someone would turn to look at a tombstone – a father, a son, a wife – and walk on to the new one. When they came to the waiting gap in the earth a woman started sobbing and tears that were held back were suddenly released. Rina came and stood near him and he could not bear her closeness. Yoram's mother met his eyes and he felt she knew. The ceremony was short and simple. The shrouded body was lowered and a shiver went through Daniel's spine as it touched the mud. Lumps of wet earth engulfed the body shamelessly and the coarse weeping of young soldiers broke the silence at last. ' Dust unto dust, the Lord gave and the Lord has taken, blessed be the Lord . . . ' The empty words filled the valley with accusation and the first drops of rain blessed this new acquisition of the hungry earth. Yoram was covered with layers and layers, never to emerge smiling again, and the memory of his laughter sent more tears from the red eyes of the villagers to mix with rain-drops. Someone led Yoram's mother away and the others followed, sending back looks of disbelief, walking faster as they descended as if there, down below in an open jeep, Yoram was waiting to prove them wrong.

Daniel stayed with Rina, not looking at her until they could hear the sound of car-engines and see the cars and tractors entering Gilad.

' You're crying,' she said. Her eyes were dry.

' It's the rain,' he murmured.

' I'm cold.' She was shivering.

He put his jacket round her thin shoulders sensing her tremble as he did so. She looked at the flowers on the fresh grave and shrugged.

' We'd better go,' he said.

She nodded. She walked ahead of him and he noticed her dress which was gray flannel and her yellow patterned scarf which slipped to her shoulders and her thin black cardigan. He remembered their walks back from school reading Gorky and reciting Pushkin and he remembered her hard lips pleading for warmth and love which he could not give. He tried to reconstruct Yoram's lips and was unable to. Yoram's nose, Yoram's hands, his shoulders, his voice. Could Rina remember him? All that was left was the smile in the eyes – he could not recall their colour or Yoram's funny walk. He tried to remember things Yoram said to him and the horror of not remembering made him stop. Rina didn't look back and when he caught up with her she asked :

' Why did you stop on the way? '

' What was the colour of his eyes? ' he asked.

She almost smiled.

124

'You don't remember, do you? It will all creep back. The eyes and the voice and the words and the expressions. Not when you expect or even want it, so leave him in peace now.'

The rain stopped and the sky darkened. The wind grew stronger and the little jeep was a welcome shelter.

They were driving slowly towards the main road.

'And now?' she asked.

'Where would you like to go?' He wasn't looking at her.

'I think back to Jerusalem. You can leave me anywhere and I'll get the bus.'

'I'll take you there. I want to go to Yoram's parents first and then take a few things from my room.'

There was commotion in front of the little room. People went in and out and the door was left open like on wedding-days. A few people shook Daniel's hand in sympathy and he walked past them into the room. On the divan Yoram's parents were sitting still and shy as if apologetic for finding themselves the centre of attention. A few relatives Daniel had never seen before were occupying the chairs and Yoram's picture framed in black was on the small table. Daniel approached them holding his beret and wondering what to say or do. Yoram's mother looked up at him and began to cry. He felt tears run down his cheeks and there was nothing more to say. Between them lay the amputated body and the bridge of tears was sufficient. He looked at Yoram's father who stood up and embraced him gently and when leaving Daniel said:

'I'll bring the rest of his things from the camp.'

There was a little kerosene stove in the room, but somehow the fresh air felt warmer. Rina was sitting in the jeep waiting and he knew she preferred not to go in.

125

' Where are you off to? ' someone asked.

' Jerusalem,' he said, turning the jeep away from the house, from Gilad, from the cemetery and the river.

He missed his watch. He had lost his sense of time because he felt no hunger and the accumulated fatigue of days did not signal approaching bed time. The noise of the engine prevented conversation and when they stopped in Tel-Aviv for coffee he felt a sudden attraction to the big city. He could bury himself in its glitter and smell its new smells and feed on new tastes and shapes and meanings. The Jordan was now as far away as the Vistula and he had no home once again and smiling for the first time in many days he felt a strange sensation of freedom. They headed east into the hills as the sun was setting in the west behind them. The intimacy of the winding mountain road made Rina think aloud and he knew he need not worry about her. He felt a chill as they climbed towards the lights of Jerusalem, and for the last few kilometres he had the strange sensation of not driving at all but rather being pulled by the big magnetic clasps of the city.

It was early but the streets were deserted. A few people could be seen, heavily clad, hurrying for shelter and drops of rain glittered on the rough stone surfaces of the buildings. The city looked underlit and he drove slowly as if trying not to disturb the eternal sleep of holy ghosts. He left Rina in front of an old house where she shared a room with another student and said a quick good night. There was nothing to say. For a minute the pride was gone from her face and she turned to go, humble and yielding.

He parked the jeep and walked along a narrow street in the religious quarter. His own footsteps echoed towards the sleeping wall, the border, the other Jerusalem. All the windows had shutters and only when he passed the large

Yeshiva building could be heard a vague human sound, a monotonous incantation of prayers which the wind tossed into the air, turning it into a wailing cry. It meant nothing to Daniel though the strange sound sent a shiver through his spine. He tightened his battle jacket and tried to concentrate and think of his father. His thoughts chased each other madly, deliberately avoiding Yoram's fresh grave and he reached the end of the street where a border sign made him turn back.

Moonless night, starless night, and all the roads were blocked suddenly. He could not go to battle again, he had no desire to return to Gilad, Nechama's body knew too much and somewhere on another continent there was a man he did not know who claimed his love. He would tend to Kalinsky first he thought, and drove to the Jerusalem camp where he could spend the night.

There was something awkward about Daniel the next morning. Used to open fields or the army atmosphere of excitement and informality he was lost in the corridors of the Jewish Agency looking for his file. People were sitting on benches patiently waiting to find solutions to life-long riddles. He was told to wait outside and two women pointed to the bench where he obediently occupied the offered seat.

' Are you looking for someone you've lost? ' the older one asked.

' I've found them,' he said casually.

' You're a lucky man,' said the younger woman. ' Did it take years?'

' Yes,' he said, attempting to put an end to the unwelcome exchange.

' The thing is not to lose hope,' said the first woman. ' I've been looking for my boy for twenty years now.'

He looked at her. Her hair was white but her face unwrinkled. She was dressed in black and there was a wedding ring on her finger. He could not help thinking of his mother, the way he remembered her. Her hair would never turn white in his memory, her face would remain radiant and smooth and beautiful, her body lush and young. They called his name.

Horowitz sent him to Levy and Levy gave him the file and told him to go to another room, to Rosenberg, and he ended in front of a middle-aged man behind a steel desk.

He had no reason to feel belligerent, yet he did. Something in those faces disturbed him. They had a patient kindness. Their looks indicated an effort to get involved, to display human understanding, to show care, and yet there was saturation in their weary eyes. They had heard too much, they had seen it all, they were witnesses to the greatest joys and even greater tragedies and they were touched too often. Somewhere along the shelves loaded with files they had acquired a horrible sense of proportion. They knew what really mattered, they were detached from the small distresses, they were taken, perhaps unqualified, through labyrinths which should be closed to strangers and their eyes reflected the superior knowledge of the profoundest of sources.

'You're a lucky man,' the clerk said.

'A woman outside said the same,' Daniel remarked thoughtlessly.

'They are still waiting for a visa, but it's easier now. Have they decided to immigrate?'

'I have to find out about conditions, jobs, a place to live in – things like that.'

'Couldn't they stay with you in the Kibbutz?'

He tried to picture Gilad but could produce only an

enlarged view of the cemetery hill.

'They could try it, but I doubt if they would care for it much. Kalinsky is a merchant.'

'You mean your father? I see. There are some shops in Beer-Sheba, and we shall take care of him at the beginning. He can get a small house there on good terms and learn Hebrew. The other big towns are more difficult right now.'

He thought of the flowers in Nechama's room, of the dust along the main road, of the wild camels and the market day.

'I'll write him and let you know.'

The men gave him some forms to fill in, and watched him tensely.

'Have you been fighting in the Sinai?'

'Yes, sort of.'

'If only I were younger! But they kept me here. Civil Defence job. I used to be of better use.' He smiled at Daniel who shook hands with him and left.

The sun was out now but it was brisk and cold and he had nothing to do in the city. He called on Rina to find with a sense of relief that she was out and he went to a café crowded with students to write a letter to his father. The first few lines were matter-of-fact; Beer-Sheba, a house, a shop, a new language, difficulties to overcome. Then, forgetting who the letter was addressed to, he wrote of Yoram. 'We buried my best and only friend yesterday, he died an unnecessary stupid death. With him,' he wrote, 'died many things for me and I am not sure what I'll do next or where I shall be. I am going to leave the army and perhaps leave Gilad. I owed everything that was good in my life to Yoram and I shall never be able to pay the debt.' He wrote about Rina, Yoram's girl and about Yoram's parents and for the first time ended the letter

' with love '. When he posted it he regretted having written it and wondered how it would sound in Polish.

There were things to be done, and he was fortunate. He had to go back south and check with the unit, he had to find out about houses in Beer-Sheba, he had to get Yoram's things from camp. Driving south, towards a warmer sun, he began to realize how much things had changed; he had never asked himself questions before. He accepted what befell him, at times gratefully, at times taking it for granted. The monotony of the road south reminded him of his hunger and need for sleep and when he arrived at camp in the afternoon he went to his room, stopping off in the kitchen briefly and fell asleep fully dressed until the following morning.

Two weeks later, still undecided what to do next, he received a reply from Kalinsky.

He found a translator – he hated the thought of one person translating all the letters as if they were a serialized family story and preferred strangers to acquaintances – and listened carefully.

They would come, if conditions were right. A long list of questions followed, mostly to do with finance and exchange rates and details he knew nothing about. How many rooms would the proposed house have and what about high-school for Miriam? Would she have to serve in the army? How hot was Beer-Sheba and would it be possible to get something for them in Tel-Aviv? They heard the south was desert and waterless. What kind of goods could they bring in order to sell, was land speculation profitable? The last few lines referred to Yoram. Kalinsky ' was sorry to hear of Yoram's death, but that is the way wars are and think of the world war disaster,' he added, ' we could have all been lost.'

White days, white nights, nurses in white on Lipsky's terrace, white shrouds, the window. He would go and visit Rina, but perhaps he should not go anywhere, not even afterwards. He could sit at the window and look down and watch the living brought in and the dead taken out. He kept Kalinsky's letter about Yoram. We could have all been lost, it said, as if we weren't. Although he never talked to him about it, he wanted to wave it in his father's face, and ask him where Shmuel was and his mother? Who was saved? A man who lost his dignity many times along the road to salvation and gave up his child. That is the way wars are, Kalinsky. How true and how profound, but who chooses? Who bestows upon one the courage to go forward and upon the other stupidity to let him do so, who selects the parents who will cry on the square flat tombstone? Yes, father, you can speculate in land, many do, you can bring goods and sell them, you can have a shop and your house had three rooms and Miriam didn't serve in the army because she married before her conscription was due and I started asking questions and not liking the answers I got.

Think of the war disaster, you wrote me, as if it was subject to thought, or self-pity or description of any kind. When they took me away from you they kept me for three months before I ran away and was hidden in the village. Did I ever tell you what these three months were like? Can I remember? They defy memory the way they defy pity or thought, they even defy dreams. My life began in Bari, I was born in Bari on a boat and I grew up in Gilad and all that happened before Bari should be erased from my brain and conscience. You brought to me the years

131

I happily lost, from the first moment we met and during every moment afterwards. Do you remember our first meeting? Did you know how much I waited for that moment, how my hands trembled and my forehead perspired? When I drove to the port of Haifa that day thinking of Yoram's parents, how they had lost someone far better than the son you were about to find, I could see the boat in the distance, in the dawn.

Chapter Eight

The boat emerged from the morning mist, larger than expected, slower and whiter. It was floating on a cushion of fog and for a brief moment Daniel wished it would turn away, like a dream and back slowly to where it belonged, leaving only a vague trace in his memory. Instead it approached steadily and the small pilot boat manoeuvred it to the dock.

He found himself standing on the quay among others and although there was nothing peculiar about him he felt he was being stared at. He fumbled in his pockets for some papers and entered the small Jewish Agency office.

' Are they going to go directly to Beer-Sheba? ' he was asked.

' How should I know? '

' How long has it been since you saw your father? '

' Twenty-one years.'

' I'd better come with you and help you find him. They may want to go with you to the Kibbutz for a few days, it might make it easier for them.'

' It's all right.'

' How will you speak to them? '

' I don't know. I speak only Hebrew.'

' Don't worry,' the man said. ' Most of the people on

the quay are waiting for people they haven't seen for years. For some it's the very first meeting. After the first few moments it's usually all right.'

Daniel was wearing dark blue cotton trousers and brown shoes. His white shirt was creased at the back from driving and a slight pressure in his stomach made him feel sick.

'I'll find you in a few moments,' the man said and Daniel joined the others.

The boat was parallel to the quay now and large letters announced its name and purpose, *Moledet* (Homeland). It carried a few tourists, Israelis returning from vacations abroad and three hundred immigrants from Eastern Europe. Women nervously beautified themselves, holding mirrors in trembling hands to cover with powder and lipstick the marks left by twenty years, hoping to resemble childhood snapshots which people were holding in their hands in order to identify relatives. Next to where he stood a large family surrounded a very old man who was crying. Daniel watched with nervous intensity, there was something weird about the old man crying, as if the old shrunken body held no water any more and the tears were the last liquids in the shrivelled man, produced with great effort, drying him up to a skeleton. The old man was helped closer to the water, his eyes dry now, and a girl next to him was told to wave to the passengers.

'But I don't see anybody,' she said.

'It doesn't matter, they see you.'

It made Daniel shiver. They see me, he thought. Suppose they know and recognize me, and they are waving and I am standing here glued to the cold asphalt with my face pale and expressionless. He tried to smile and lift his hand but the people on the deck seemed one immense blackness, a faceless entity of misery and homelessness.

134

Someone grabbed his arm and he jerked aside. It was an excited woman who gestured to the deck, crying and mumbling.

' My mother,' she said, ' my mother is there! '

Stupidly he asked: ' Where? ' and the woman did not answer and let go of his arm.

' There,' she said, ' with the others! '

So is my father, he thought and now he looked at the faces, each one becoming crystal clear as they were screened by his gray eyes and dismissed as unlikely to bear the name Kalinsky.

The gangway was lifted and he looked for the official who promised to help him. He was a young man with an old expression and he held a plastic briefcase under his arm. When he caught Daniel's eye he came nearer.

' Shall we go? ' he asked.

' I'd better wait here. When you see them can you just tell them I'm here, waiting.'

' As you wish.'

People were disembarking carrying bundles and suitcases and Daniel hid behind the canteen car which provided the visitors with cold drinks and sandwiches. He could sneak out now, he thought, through the other gate, to his car and drive away. He could go south where they would never find him or north to a small village or work on a ship for a while until he could face them, at least until he could talk to them. A man was walking towards him, rather tall and fair and smoking a pipe. He was well-dressed and carried a leather suitcase. For a second Daniel's heart leaped, it could be Kalinsky, but he realized the man was only ten years his senior. How old is Kalinsky he wondered? thinking about the old man who had just used up his last tears. He watched the children being guided down, it was their Bari trip, he thought and there was no Yoram around to sing a song to them. He thought of Shmuel. Did his father wish then that it was Shmuel waiting for him?

Then he saw them kiss. He had never seen people kiss that way, consuming each other, embracing each other as if death was next door waiting to tear them apart again and suddenly the whole quay was a scene of tears and kisses and hugs. When did he kiss last, he thought, and remembered Rina's thin hard lips and Nechama's lush mouth. He had never embraced a man, never kissed a stranger, is he going to have to kiss Kalinsky? The officials watched proudly. The tears of joy and the reunited families embracing were their achievement. When one of them wiped a tear it was a shy sentimental one, and occasionally a strong healthy porter could be seen doing the same.

The big clock above the customs house indicated the hours. It was earlier than Daniel imagined and he felt hungry. It would be ludicrous meeting my father munching a sandwich he thought. A young family of Israelis returning home disembarked. They were kissed lightly by a relative and proceeded chatting to the customs house talking about the beauty of Florence, already sharing the acquired experiences. Rumanian, Yiddish, Polish, a porter swearing in Arabic, a child weeping. Perhaps they were not on this boat, he thought, looking at the people descending, none of whom resembled any of his notions of his family's looks.

Then he saw the official. He felt his hands covered with sweat and put them in his pockets fumbling with the small change he carried. The official pointed to a group of people coming down now and Daniel couldn't see a thing. The boat, the gangway, the dark on white letters saying *Moledet,* the crowded quay were all blurred now and he could not move. It was not that he was crying, because he was, but his whole body was crying. The tears did not just stream down his cheeks, his eyes were heavy with them and he was choking on them and there were tears thinning his blood making him feel feeble and unstable and he was six years old again and left alone searching for his father. Through the tears he watched them coming towards him and it did not matter now whether Kalinsky was short or tall or thin or young or anything he ever imagined him to be. There was his father, his step-mother, his step-sister and he was not alone for a moment and he was not a brave soldier or a tough farmer or a charming young man or an Israeli patriot, he was again Daniel Kalinsky from Warsaw, son of Haim Kalinsky.

They stopped now. He still could not see them clearly, although there was only a few feet between him and the group. The official fumbled for words and said in Yiddish to Kalinsky:

'This is Daniel, your son, I'd better leave you alone.' And to Daniel in Hebrew:

'This is your father and his family. I'll look for you later.'

Kalinsky was the one to take the few steps towards his son. First he shook his hand which Daniel never remembered taking out of his pocket, then they embraced. Daniel closed his eyes and felt the man trembling with sobs mumbling his name and a few words of joy. Dora joined them and kissed him and the little girl, who was really a young woman, stood rather shyly and watched them. He noticed how small the man in his arms was and when he opened his eyes all he could see was his father's

137

thin hair and shabby coat-collar. He had a strange unfamiliar smell, similar to winter clothes brought out of trunks, and in one hand he was still holding a bundle tied with rope. Daniel gently pushed his father away and looked at him. The man was smiling now, touching his son's strong arm and feeling him the way a blind man gets acquainted with a new object.

Daniel said, ' *Aba* ' (Father) and the man started crying again. He watched the man crying and something happened inside him. Suddenly, it was all over. The excitement, the expectations, the trembling, the worries. There was the small man facing him with his small eyes and exhausted expression, and he was a stranger. He could address him as *Aba,* he could let him kiss his cheek, but he was a little man from Poland, a ghost from an unknown past, a burden. He had a duty to fulfil, the same sense of responsibility that prompted Yoram to do volunteer work, but nothing more. There were three people in need and he was going to help them to settle and be rehabilitated but he looked into the man's eyes, detached and aloof now, and he found nothing there which he remembered or knew. Miriam was standing nearby, suspicious and remote, and he gave her his hand which she shook politely. He touched her hair lightly and took the bundle she was carrying. She thanked him in Hebrew. Of course, he remembered, she spoke some Hebrew by now, which made the trip to Gilad or Beer-Sheba seem less terrifying. He asked them to follow and on their way they met the official.

' Where will you be going? ' he asked, giving Daniel an envelope of documents for his father.

' Ask my father,' Daniel responded dully. They exchanged a few phrases in Yiddish and the official translated:

'They don't mind. He would like to be with you, see where and how you live and then go on to his new place. He did not realize Beer-Sheba was so many miles from Gilad.'

They had five small suitcases, all their belongings. The girl had a bundle of personal things in addition and Haim carried a parcel which was square and heavy. Daniel loaded the car and asked them to wait for a moment. He went to the canteen and bought a few sandwiches and some beer and brought it back to them. He was hungry now but when his father watched him eat he felt he could not swallow and for many miles wondered how to dispose of the half-eaten sandwich he was holding in his left hand. When he left he told the secretary of Gilad he might be bringing them along for a few days and a room had been allotted to them not far from where Daniel lived. On the way Miriam did most of the talking, asking about the different places they passed and quickly translating the brief answers. Towards lunch-time he took the familiar turn to the village and he felt his father touch his arm and say with a strange accent:

'Gilad!'

It was a Thursday, not yet summer although spring was over and people were at work. The pleasant silence of midday produced a sense of emptiness and they did not meet anybody on their way to the room. The car was unloaded and as Dora did not like the idea of letting Miriam stay apart from them he went to arrange for a third bed to be brought, leaving his family to unpack and shower. When he returned he found himself smiling at the chaos created in the little room. Clothes on the bed, a fur stole airing on the window sill, cans of food on the floor, a few books, papers, some old toys of Miriam's who surely didn't play with dolls any more but had brought them over for sentimental reasons. It all felt like winter introduced in a summer resort.

'You will need some light summer clothes,' Daniel suggested.

'We'll see, we'll see,' said Kalinsky, a phrase he used very often, postponing decisions and avoiding commitments.

Now that he took off his jacket his son realized how weak he must be. His arms were thin and white and his stomach fallen. He could see the veins on the back of the transparent hands and could not believe the same blood flowed in his. He looked at Dora now but when his eyes caught hers he turned away. He was embarrassed by his curiosity. He had no right to look into the contents of their bundles and cases. The square parcel, he discovered, had boxes of cigars, for sale Haim explained later, and one case contained kitchen utensils, some towels and sheets, a feather blanket.

'They had to leave everything behind,' said the girl. 'They had many things, they gave them away.' The girl, he thought, she is all right.

'Shall I take you for a walk? '

She smiled in gratitude, there was no room for her to sit down in the cramped space, and she didn't know what to do. When she told her parents she was going out with Daniel they said they would come along too, and see Gilad.

'We'll have lunch first,' he snapped.

'Is there a restaurant here? '

'There is a dining room.'

He sat them down at a table, exposed to the kind looks

of others, and went to look for someone who could speak their language. He didn't have to go far because one of the people he had in mind had just entered and, as if a burden had been lifted off him, he enjoyed seeing his father get involved in conversation. Yaskov, the man who spoke Polish, was smiling and at times laughing, the way you laugh at a child who asks foolish but charming questions. He turned to Daniel.

' He wants to know if you'll come with him to Beer-Sheba, if you can leave Gilad? '

' Tell him I will help him for a while and then return here.'

If he were to tell the truth he would have said, ' Tell him this is home, and there will never be another, with or without family. Tell him the foreignness will have to disappear first, the smell, the gold tooth, the whiteness, the long Polish words, the cigars, those clothes, those shoes, the suspicion in his eyes, the smallness of his eyes. Tell him I am unfair, expecting him to be twenty-five years younger, an adaptable enthusiastic young man, tell him I want to be proud of my father and I shall wait until he gives me a reason to be.' Instead he said:

' I'm proud of him. It must have been difficult to decide to leave.'

This was translated and Haim smiled. He said:

' Tell him I came because of him.'

They wanted to go for a walk but Daniel suggested it would be too hot until the late afternoon. They should rest, he suggested, and on the way back to their house he showed them his room and a few minutes later he was left alone.

' We'll see, we'll see ', Kalinsky said after every sentence. What was there to see? He did not feel

141

responsible for them, yet he was. He was no longer alone, yet he felt lonelier than ever. He took a shower and lay on his back, tense and tired, wondering if Yoram would have made any difference. Perhaps he could find Rina, she might be there for the week-end, perhaps she could help him think. There was nothing to think about. The Kalinskys would have to go to Beer-Sheba, the Agency had prepared everything, and the rest is time and some understanding. A light knock on his door made him jump.

' Come in,' he said, almost shouting the welcome phrase.

It was Miriam. She entered and immediately turned away. He noticed he was wearing only his shorts and quickly slipped into slacks and a shirt.

' What is it? ' he asked.

She shrugged.

' Nothing.'

He asked her to sit and she obeyed looking at the books on the table. Her face lit up when she could read the name Mayakovsky on one of the volumes.

' Do you know the poems? '

' Yes,' she said. ' The one about the sun.'

She had a way of looking at him, a way she did not change for many years after that first day, and he lowered his eyes. As if she understood and accused without demanding an answer or an explanation.

' Where is Yoram? ' she said. She had a photograph he had sent a long time ago. It was a snapshot of him and Yoram laughing.

' They never told you? ' he asked.

She shook her head.

' Let's go out,' he said.

They walked along the pavement, stopping to greet some people who turned back to watch them walking on, and left the village away from the river to climb the hill.

' Yoram is dead,' he said. ' He was killed in the war.'

She was not familiar with the word killed but dead she understood.

' You have a friend now? ' she asked.

' No.'

They climbed the cemetery hill and looked at the valley coloured by a pastel sunset. Although the flowers were dead and the wheat turned yellow the air had softness which mellowed the colours. She drank in the beauty and suddenly she was crying and laughing. ' Moledet,' she said. She must have learned Hebrew from a very enthusiastic patriot, because her vocabulary was full of words, old-fashioned and used only cynically in the country, like homeland, promised land, the return to Sion, the conquest of the desert, melting-pot and the like.

' Yes,' he said, very moved, ' Moledet. Here is Gilad, and there is Shimron with its red roofs reflecting the sun-beams, and that is the northern road to the Lebanese border.'

She asked about the fish ponds and she wanted to see an orange tree, When they walked by the cemetery she insisted on going in. She had never seen a cemetery and reluctantly he guided her to Yoram's flat tombstone. She took out the photograph and had tears in her eyes.

' Do you cry often? ' he asked, almost cruelly.

' Never,' and she looked at him in a way which made him wish he hadn't even asked the question.

She read the letters on the marble stone and bent down to uproot a weed.

' Let's go back to your parents,' he said.

The room was crowded with people to his surprise. The cook had brought in a cake and Rivka brought some flowers in a vase. All the Polish speaking members of Gilad were there, five or six of them, asking about Warsaw, about families they used to know, about streets and the river and the parks and the monuments with more pride in the fact that they remembered than eagerness to obtain new information. Haim and Dora seemed comfortable and Daniel, slightly jealous and definitely an outsider in all the commotion, stretched on the square of lawn outside with Miriam next to him.

' Where is the river? ' she asked.

' Down there,' he lazily pointed out a direction.

' Can I go there? '

' Yes, but don't be late, we shall have supper soon.'

She took off her shoes and socks, noticing that many of the villagers walked barefooted and stepping slowly sensing the rough soil for the first time, disappeared behind the houses. People were leaving the room, it was almost time to go to dinner and Dora changed into a light flowery dress. Haim asked for Miriam and Daniel explained she had gone to the river, to the Jordan. Awkwardly Haim pantomimed a soldier and said, ' Arabs, boom boom,' referring to the possibility of danger in walking alone. Daniel laughed it off, using the word Miriam had used. ' Moledet,' he said, ' ours,' and spread his arms to indicate it was all ours, safe, comfortable, home. Kalinsky nodded and mumbled something. Daniel thought he said something about Yoram but he preferred not to ask.

When they returned from the dining room, and Miriam was awaiting them, rosy-cheeked and apparently happy, Dora insisted on opening a tin. It had pears in syrup, large and pale and sugary. She took out a spoon and made him eat one. He never liked tinned fruit and these were topped with some chocolate which his father had kept. It must

144

have been a good piece of chocolate but for some reason it felt stale in Daniel's mouth and he excused himself, said goodnight and went to his room.

And in his room Rina was waiting. He had written to her some time earlier, a vague perfunctory letter mentioning the date of his family's arrival, and she had come to see him. After Yoram's death Rina had completed her studies and her life-long romance with the thin decorative Nabataean ceramics had begun. She lived in Jerusalem, kept a room in Beer-Sheba and came for week-ends to Shimron and Gilad, somehow taking Yoram's place in his parents' agonized existence. Yoram's death had changed her face and her attitudes, but somehow isolated her from the passage of time and one had the feeling she was doomed to look forever the way she looked in the rain on cemetery hill a few years back. She was friendless and yet a friend to others and the same intensity with which she ignored the future marked her passionate attitude to the past. She took off her sandals and her hair was still wet from the shower she had taken a few minutes earlier.

' Have they arrived? '

' Very much so.'

' Don't be belligerent. Would you rather I left? '

'No, you can stay. Your tall blond man is a short hairless thin stranger, that's all.'

And silence. Rina never endured silence for long, not because she feared it but because she regarded it as a waste of time.

' Did you recognize them? '

' No. Someone introduced us. Very formal it was.'

' Did you kiss and cry? ' There was no sarcasm in her question, nor curiosity. She wished to be told the facts, in detail. She wanted to reconstruct the scene which she had imagined for so long.

' No,' he lied to her. Perhaps he was lying to her for the first and last time in his life. ' Forget the stories you hear or imagine. We shook hands and we couldn't talk and I doubt if we would have had anything to talk about even if we had a language in common. The girl is nice, Kalinsky is not much to look at and as for Dora, well, you'll see her. They should never have come here and I should never have made them take the trip.'

' All this after one day? You already know him and know what is best for him? Perhaps you should try to remember that he *is* your father. What made you think it was going to be different, or easier? Isn't it up to you now? '

' Look, I don't feel like being preached to. They are here, and I shall take them to Beer-Sheba and see them settled and I am not impatient or demanding. They have a peculiar smell – even the young girl.'

Rina's face became redder than ever, the freckles disappearing. Her long fingers clutched the arms of the chair and she looked as though she wanted to hit him.

' Where do you think you came from? Perhaps you smelled the same way when you arrived in Gilad, before the sun and the dust and the river smoothed your skin and made you smell of clover and orange blossoms. What do you think Yoram died for if not to give a little Kalinsky an alternative to Ghetto life? '

' My God! ' he yelled, standing up now. ' You too! Yoram died because I was foolish. Don't drag him into it. Kalinsky came because I was foolish. He asked if there was a restaurant here and he brought cigars to sell! '

' So you want them all to arrive knowing the Kibbutz

code by heart, and you want him to live off the air and the view. I hope he can sell his cigars and I wish Gilad had a restaurant. I'm going to see them now.'

'When Yoram died he wrote me and said that's the way wars are!'

'You don't have to be cruel. If you're not coming I'll go alone.'

She put on her sandals and he fumbled for words of apology.

'I'm sorry. I suppose I'm embarrassed and confused as they must be. Let's go.'

There was a light on in the little room and voices could be heard. A half-moon rested on top of the berry tree behind the house and he noticed the buds on the rose bushes. He knocked on the door and heard a foreign word in reply. They were sitting as if they were expecting someone. Dora was wearing a long dressing gown, but her hair was pulled up and freshly combed. Miriam was reading a Hebrew book and Haim had his jacket on. Rina introduced herself and shook their hands, pausing to hold Haim's with both her hands.

'What were you doing?' she asked Miriam.

'Nothing. Waiting. They wanted to talk to Daniel but didn't want to disturb him, so we were just sitting.'

'Tell them Daniel is very happy they are here. Tell them we all are.'

Rina was getting into one of her moods. She would have liked it all to happen immediately. She was ready to give them their first Hebrew lesson, to show them the whole country that night, to read them her favourite Hebrew pieces, to dress them up as Sabras and see Miriam dance the Hora. She was talking fast and the girl did not seem to follow.

147

'It will be difficult at the beginning. Beer-Sheba is not Gilad, it is hot and dry and sandy and colourless but when my parents immigrated this whole valley was a marshland. Tell them any effort will pay and they are young enough and healthy and they can make the effort.'

Kalinsky wanted to know what Rina did.

'I'm an archaeologist,' she explained.

He asked what her salary was like. Daniel blushed and said curtly:

'What does it matter?'

Rina told him what she earned and smiled. 'Not too bad,' she added. 'And I come to Beer-Sheba often so I'll see you there and be your shop's first and best customer.'

There was nothing much to add to her enthusiastic speech.

'You must be tired,' she said.

'Yes,' Dora answered.

'And in Warsaw, in the evening, what did you do?'

Dora's face lightened.

'We had many friends, even some Goyim. We would sit and talk, sometimes play cards, have some tea and go to sleep quite early. Do you think we could get some tea here?' she asked Miriam.

Rina went out of the room to try and find an electric kettle and Daniel remained, looking at his father.

'Rina is right,' he said. 'It's not going to be easy, not knowing people at the beginning.'

Kalinsky fumbled for his wallet and brought out a piece of paper.

'It's a friend of his,' Miriam explained, 'a rabbi. He lives in Jerusalem now, he would like to visit him if it is possible.'

'Of course. We'll all go to Beer-Sheba and when you are

ready for a trip, after a few days, I'll take you to him.'

He didn't recognize the address but he knew it was somewhere in the religious quarter.

' Or you could write him to come and visit you.'

' His child is sick, he doesn't travel,' Miriam volunteered.

Rina returned triumphantly. She carried an electric kettle, some tea and sugar and cups and placed them on the table as if proving conclusively that everything was possible and obtainable in Israel. She taught them the Hebrew words for good-night, which made Kalinsky very happy, and they left the room.

' Would you drive me back? '

' We can walk, if you're not too tired.'

She held Daniel's arm, which irritated him, and they chose the short cut through the fields. The night was cool and damp and mist hovered above the fish ponds. They walked through the frog-grass and listened to the packs of jackals howling, seeking prey.

' It's like a test for you,' she said. ' Something to cope with, something important.'

He did not answer.

' Listen to the frogs,' he said. ' What a hateful sound.'

' They seem very nice. Simple, willing, quite adaptable.'

' Not enough rain this year,' he said, looking at the wheat.

' All right. I won't mention them. You can use my room in Beer-Sheba when you are there if you prefer it to their house and leave their address on my table when you leave.'

' Thank God they're not Orthodox,' he said.

Very few lights were on in Shimron. He did not go into the village with her but turned to go at a crossroad.

' I wish we were back at school,' he smiled now.

' And Yoram alive,' she sighed, not really addressing

149

him. ' Take care of them. And of yourself.'

He enjoyed the walk back. He wished he could walk on and on like that, never quite leaving Shimron, never making it to Gilad, haunted by the sounds of night and using his senses rather than his mind.

Haim and Dora enjoyed their tea and Miriam was reading aloud to them, trying to teach them a few words. The three small beds were placed along the walls and when Miriam was asleep Haim whispered to Dora.

' Do you think he likes me? '

' Of course he does, he is your son.'

' He looks like his mother.'

' He's very good-looking, and I like his girl, I think she's kind.'

' I wish I could talk to him, alone, fluently.'

' You soon will. *Laila Tov,* (good-night),' she said, smiling at her own accent.

None of them slept much that first night. Miriam was awake and for the first time was aware of a question which had never bothered her before – did she love her father? She expected her half-brother to be different, she thought he would take her in his arms and lift her as if she were a baby and make her laugh. She liked the laughing face of his friend in the picture and all that was left of him was the marble stone she dared not touch. Haim felt fear. He wished the bed was larger and the child away and he wanted to be nearer Dora. He was afraid, like a passenger who has taken the wrong train, and yet there was no other train to take and this was the end of a trip. He rather liked the green smells that invaded the room and he was proud of his son. Dora was uncomfortable in her narrow bed and was wondering whether to go to the distant lavatory or leave it until the morning. She did not

150

care much. She wanted Haim to be happy, she wanted Miriam to marry and have children, she was bound to make a few friends and soon settle into a new routine. She was worried about Daniel, he looked like a boy and she knew he would never be her son, perhaps never be Haim's son either. Daniel was tortured by guilt and once again swore to make an effort. Of course Rina was right. Kalinsky's arrival was what it was all about and there was no way of dismissing it. Time alone could not do miracles, and he would have to help it happen. He thought of Nechama, he would have liked a woman near him, and he even thought of Rina's long limbs as he fell asleep.

Chapter Nine

And now he is dying, Daniel thought to himself, standing
by the window, and the miracle never quite happened.
Like those plants, grown up north and then transplanted
south, they don't die but the sand absorbs the water and
the salt eats into the roots and they degenerate until they
hardly resemble their brothers in the fertile north. They
exist, that's all, and you managed an existence in Beer-
Sheba, you still do. The first day, the first week, month,
year, five years, the roots never dug their way deeper and
the branches never reached very high. You reached the
waist of reality and lived a dwarfish life, a miniature of a
life. And you knew it.

Bending down saved Kalinsky from collapsing and his
frequent complaints became a habit, a form of self-
indulgence rather than a demand on anybody. The house
was not a new one but it was large enough and with a loan
they managed to furnish it. The shop was a sort of
general store and it served a suburban area and saved
people the long and tiring trip to the more glamorous
shops in the centre. In the Jewish Agency file the Kalinsky
family was categorized as absorbed, economically independent and socially integrated. Daniel stayed with them
for a few days and realized his father could manage the

shop on his own without any help from him. He had a quick mind when it came to purchasing goods, and things which Daniel would judge as useless and tasteless sold very well. When the first customers arrived Kalinsky asked them for their names, and their husbands' professions and Dora talked to them about their children. Daniel, embarrassed and angry, kept quiet, having to control himself whenever his name was brought up.

' Why do you have to talk to them? Can't they buy whatever they need, pay for it and leave? '

' They enjoy it. They want the attention, they're curious about us too, it's natural.'

He avoided arguing with Kalinsky and when he was asked with a knowing smile about Rina, something about marrying her, grandchildren and the like, he merely said:

' She's not my girl. She was going to marry Yoram, we're just friends.'

' So when will you get married? '

They always meant well and he always misinterpreted it as prying, as pettiness, as an imposition.

When he left them in Beer-Sheba he returned to Gilad, promising to take them to Jerusalem a few weeks later and Rina, who saw them often, kept reminding him. She also kept repeating things his father said, about politics, about the Arabs, about his neighbours, the heat, the dust, the language.

' What am I supposed to do? '

' Nothing. I don't think he's very happy and you could at least visit more often.'

' Oh no, I can't.'

And he didn't. It was not a rational dislike. It had to do with details, with the sight of the old clock which never worked, the shabby bed covers they had brought with them from Poland still bearing that peculiar smell of another world. It had to do with a plastic rose they placed on the book shelf in a yellow vase and the stuffy little shop with strangers entering and exiting, discussing their ailments and asking for credit.

Miriam had a boy friend, the son of some newly-made friends who were helping his father in some business or another and he disliked the way they encouraged her to get married, before serving in the army.

' What did you expect him to do? ' Rina asked.

' It's not the shop, it's their whole way of life. They go into the house and draw the curtains and pretend they're back in Warsaw.' And he was sure about it. He never saw them go out to see the country, just for a stroll along the main street. They never cared to know what was beyond their suburb or city, and they were not really there either. Haim would have preferred to live in Tel-Aviv but there was no possibility of a job there and the days passed, the months, the years. Daniel was not aware of their few happy moments and yet their routine was not an unhappy one.

' But what is it that bothers you about them? They seem all right,' Rina observed.

' It just doesn't work. I know they expect me to share their lives, but I can't do it. I know they don't fit, I know they'd rather return to where they came from.'

And then he decided to help them out. It was all a mistake, he figured, and it has to be faced and solved. He was going to get a job in town, for two or three months, and give his father some money and simply say – ' you can return to Warsaw if you wish.' He didn't stop to think what it would mean to start anew there, and he didn't ask them whether they cared to go back. He knew Miriam would stay and what he needed was time to save for two tickets to Warsaw, one way. The Kibbutz secretary was understanding. Rina swore not to mention it to his family and he found a very well paid temporary job as a heavy bulldozer operator.

*   *   *

Kalinsky was constantly in pain and then he felt better, as if the disease had decided to let him rest for a while and prepare him for the next blow. He lost his appetite and his decrepit body seemed to gather a new strength, independent of food or exercise, the strength of a mind, or willpower. He remained in bed now without moving and when Dora arrived in the afternoon he had a benign smile for her.

' I feel better,' he said.

She nodded. He didn't care to look at the papers and told her she should give the cake she brought to somebody else in the ward. He never mentioned the word death, but said to her:

' Perhaps afterwards, one day, you can take a trip to Jerusalem and see the rabbi. Tell him I thought of him a great deal.'

As usual she left earlier than the other visitors and he lay there in the gray light and relaxed his eyes. He was thinking about the rabbi, he was thinking about his trip to him and almost smiled when he remembered how Daniel had refused to come in.

' I'll come back for you,' he told him, ' he is your friend and you'll want to see him and talk to him alone.' And he left him there, on the threshold, and disappeared as fast as he could.

It was the saddest thing that happened to him since he

155

arrived, Haim thought. The rabbi in Warsaw never had to work and led the life of a saint surrounded by his disciples. He lived in Zamenhoffa Street and used to scold Haim for not attending services. Haim saw him before he left and promised to follow and there he was, about to visit him in a new street, a new house, in the holy city which looked so cold and small. The courtyard was crowded with children, all dressed in dark clothes wearing head-covers, their sidecurls swinging as they jumped about and cried out in Yiddish. He walked on into a small room and the rabbi's sick child was playing with a doll on the floor. The room was dark and smelly and the mongoloid girl did not pay attention to the visitor. He heard footsteps and his friend entered the room. A shy smile, a soft handshake, an apology for the lack of room and –

' Rosa, come see who is here.'

Rosa, thin and tall and gentle, asked them in and they sat in the small bedroom for tea, the child crawling about fixing Haim with a sad dumb stare. They asked each other at the same moment, ' How is life treating you,' and silence followed.

' I can't complain,' Haim finally volunteered. ' I found my son Daniel, and he is well. Miriam is happy, we manage.'

The rabbi looked older than his years, his face was white and a thin beard added paleness to his expression.

' I had to look for work. I teach now. It is difficult to make a living. Rosa wants to keep the child at home and we never lived on charity before.'

' But you are in Jerusalem.'

' A Godless city. Petty politics, one rabbi against the other, and the word of God is lost between the struggle for votes and fighting the unorthodox, but it was God's

156

will to bring me here and I shall manage. Perhaps we are not fit yet to witness the return of Zion.' He sighed. There was bitterness in his sigh.

' Do you ever pray?' he asked Haim.

' Alone, and seldom.'

' Must it be the book or the land? Can't it be both for us? '

' You are asking me, rabbi? '

' No, but I don't hear an answer.'

The child turned her head towards the door. Though mostly in silence an hour had gone by and Daniel was back. He had never been to one of those houses, had never come close to those children wearing long woollen socks and here he was, in a strange bedroom with two strange men, one of whom was his father. He shook the delicate hand of his host and felt the soft warmth melt the roughness of his own palm. He couldn't refuse the chair offered him and the rabbi sat down on the bed. The child holding her doll came nearer to him and he touched her hair. She screamed and he jumped up from his seat thinking he had hurt the girl. The rabbi did not move.

' Don't be frightened,' he said, ' she is a sick child and sometimes reacts like that.'

' I'm sorry.' Daniel looked at the girl, saliva in the corners of her mouth, her nose dripping, her hair messy. Her head was enormous and round and her eyes set in two slits. She touched his knee.

' What's her name? '

' Rachel,' he said.

' Why don't you put her in an institution? Perhaps she can be helped.'

' Rosa wants her here. She says it is God's will.'

There was no argument there, and why should he care

anyway.

' Do you ever pray my son? ' The rabbi looked at him strangely.

' In synagogue? No, I'm afraid not.'

' Alone, to thank, or to plead, or to share something? '

' I don't know.'

' Why can't we have both the book and the land,' the rabbi said, not really asking him.

' We'll have to go now,' Daniel said, standing up. The girl was touching him and he felt nauseated. ' I'll wait for you outside; Rina is waiting for me in the street,' he lied.

He hurried through the yard into the street. The aged stones were hot from absorbing the sun and he was thirsty. He felt sorry for the handsome man inside, sorry for the little girl whose face was to haunt him often, and sorry for his father who had so much looked forward to the meeting expecting to find a new king in Jerusalem and finding instead a bitter, vague, troubled man. Kalinsky came out and they walked along in silence for a while.

' I feel sorry for them,' Daniel said.

' Perhaps it *is* God's will. You should have seen him in Warsaw.'

' Why don't people like him go back? There's nothing wrong in admitting something doesn't work.'

' He'll never return. He accepts his predicament.'

Haim went to Beer-Sheba alone and Daniel returned to Tel-Aviv to start working. It was autumn.

*　　*　　*

Kalinsky refused his dinner and asked to see the doctor. He was feeling the pain again, almost hearing its heavy steps.

158

Tel-Aviv was work, it was his father's ticket, Tel-Aviv meant a change, but when he thought back on it Tel-Aviv was above all else, Nili. And when he thought of Nili he was not really thinking, because Nili could not be conceived or understood by a pure mental process. Thoughts about Nili were bells ringing wildly, butterflies colouring the field, the dizzying flights of swings in a fun fair, glittering drops of water spouting from an enormous hose to flood the world.

When he went to have lunch at the Artist's Café, still with his suitcase and with no place to spend the night, it was because he wanted a glimpse of his favourite poet who often used to sit there. He found a small table in the corner, bought an evening paper and glanced above it from time to time enjoying the commotion, half listening to strange conversations, half looking at creatures who definitely belonged to another world. He was in no hurry and the coffee was good and he decided to stay until five and then look for a room. At four o'clock Nili burst in. There was no way of ignoring her entrance. She was wearing tight slacks and a red shirt. Her flowing hair hid her face for a moment and she brushed it aside dramatically to expose a face that was all eyes. Two big blue eyes with darting, ironic pupils playing with the world, flirting with people and objects alike, inviting and rejecting at the same moment. Nili's eyes. A small nose, thin but sensuous lips and tiny, slightly flushed ears. Nili's ears. She was small and rather plump and wherever he rested his eyes, there was a curve to slip along to the next one, down to the round neat toenails. Nili's toenails. The café was half empty and for a brief moment she scanned the people in the room. 'I need help,' she declared, pleaded, commanded. 'I'm moving house! Two strong handsome

159

young men for one hour!' Ten minutes later Daniel Kalinsky was in a small attic not far from the café helping Nili move her belongings to a new flat.

Nili's belongings! There was a cage with a bird in it.

' Bobo I call it. Why Bobo? Why not? What's yours? '

' Mine? '

' Your name. Have we met before? I never remember names. Faces neither. Are you an actor or something? '

' Daniel. I'm not, are you an actress? '

' Daniel. I like that. You could have been an actor, or something. I'm a dancer, folk, for the trips abroad mainly, and soon I'll be in uniform. Say, what is this suitcase? '

' Mine.'

' Are you moving too? '

' No, just arrived.'

There were baskets with bottles and a basket with food and two suitcases and a box full of books.

' My library. I had millions but people steal them.'

When she meant one she said a dozen, ten became a thousand and a hundred was never less than a million. There was a kitbag on the floor.

' My shoes. I'm crazy about shoes, and what do you think I wear having all these fancy shoes? '

She always looked at him when she asked a question like this as if he could really answer it.

' I wear tennis-shoes and old sandals.'

There were two lampshades and a handwoven bed-cover. Three paintings and a large bunch of wild flowers.

' The flowers too. I hate a new place without flowers don't you? '

Again she looked at him for an answer.

' I suppose I do.'

160

She stopped packing.

' Are you sure we haven't met before? Where do you come from? '

' Gilad.'

' Where's that? '

' A Kibbutz, in the north, on the Jordan.'

' What are you doing here then? '

' I took a long vacation, I have to do some work here, it's a long story.'

' No, I mean here, in my room, you don't even know me, you just arrived! '

She was teasing and he blushed. She gave him her hand.

' Pleased to meet you. My name is Nili.'

There were dresses on hangers and dance costumes in a bundle.

' We can go and come back for more. The new place is just around the corner.'

They went and came back for more and he remembered his own suitcase and returned for the third time and she said :

' Come back quickly, I'm making the best coffee in Tel-Aviv, to celebrate.'

And for Nili everything was a cause for celebration.

' We have to celebrate Bobo's new place.' He nailed the cage to the wall in the kitchen. ' The first flowers in my new home! My new library! Do you like the bed under the window or opposite it? You don't talk much,' she said. ' But then I do. There is so much to say! My bottles. Where to put my bottles! ' She unpacked one of the baskets and Daniel watched her with fascination.

' I don't use them but I like to have them in the room. Some are so pretty and the names are so exotic and

161

whenever we go abroad to dance all I buy is shoes and bottles. Which scent is your favourite? '

' Orange-blossom.'

She smiled and calmed down.

' I'm not always like this. I can be serious and silent too.' But she was always like that. Even her seriousness was bubbling and her silence was that of a lightning belt. Autumn street lamps were lit and warmth settled in the corners of the little flat while she was arranging it.

' Where do you think you're going? '

' I'll look for a room.'

' You can stay here tonight,' she said. ' We can get a camp bed. I like you.'

' You can't do that,' he said. ' You're young and very pretty and the world is yours but you can't ask a stranger to stay the night just like that.'

'Aha! ' Her big eyes were serious now. ' So I can't. Well, I can and I do, and you're not a stranger and I'm not a baby and don't be so moral.'

She unpacked his suitcase and watched him shave and wash.

' It's nice to have a man in my new flat. We have to celebrate.'

* * *

He was hungry and the hospital across the road seemed to lean towards him. Its first floor was in the right place but the rest of the building, the more he looked at it, slowly tilted, stretching bare arms as if trying to reach his window. He walked down stairs to Lipsky's and ordered a sandwich. The café was empty at this hour and Mrs Lipsky wasn't there.

'She is visiting a friend across the road,' her husband explained.

Daniel's thoughts were still with Nili. She must be in the army now, dancing her way through it and missing her bottles and her shoes. He paid and walked away from the town along one of the paved roads that ended nowhere in particular.

Nili had left him in the room that first evening and returned with a camp bed and some sheets.

'Do you have money?'

'Some. Why?'

'Can we go out and have a bite, to celebrate?'

'Yes, of course.'

'I'll get dressed.' She took out three dresses and displayed them on the bed. 'Which one do you like?'

He looked at them. One was a small striped one in orange and mauve, the other two low cut and frilly, a blue and a green.

'The green one.'

'Do you have good taste?'

'How do I know?'

'I keep forgetting you come from a Kibbutz.'

'What does that have to do with it?'

'Were you born there?'

'No. I was born in Warsaw.'

She stopped combing her hair. Nili combing her hair, he could watch it the way he could watch the Jordan flowing or wheat in the wind or the dunes folding under the wheels of a car.

'Fancy me with a Pole. Can you speak Polish?'

'No.'

'I know nothing about you, do I?'

'What would you like to know?'

'The honest to God truth? Absolutely nothing. Do you mind?'

He did not mind, and it was the truth. She wanted to know nothing. She didn't care, and she wasn't curious – or rather her curiosity was limited to details.

'Your favourite colour, flower, street, dish, skirt. What's the use?' she said. 'It's all pretty words. You'll tell me you love Dostoyevsky and I will say I prefer Tolstoy and you'll tell me you are afraid of heights or women or your family and I shall analyse myself and invent complex qualities and we'll bathe in the pleasure of being profound and understanding. All I care about is that you're not a fool, and you're gorgeous-looking and you're new.'

'And when I stop being new?'

'Then off you go!' She illustrated it by waving her hand in the direction of the window. 'You'll want to, too. And no hard feelings.'

'And you'll look for something newer?'

'The way you will, the way we all do. You're here because I am new to you, and different perhaps. Not so?'

He used her evasive tactics.

'Let's go and eat. I have to go to work at five in the morning.'

'Every day?'

'For a while.'

'The green one then!'

He heard her shower and sing, he heard her dress up and sing, he heard her say good night to Bobo and she closed the shutters declaring:

'Summer is over, and that's a good excuse for celebration.'

Summer was over. Bare trees guarded the Tel-Aviv

pavements and only patterns of the neon signs gave the streets any colour. The city's pace had changed and people were hurrying indoors, thinking it was time to air the winter garments, and the birds began to wander south to hotter climates. The whitewashed houses did not reflect the sun and became as gray as the skies and at night, that night, the city looked like a heap of colourless play-bricks scattered in haste, charmless and alien. Nili was wearing her green dress and holding Daniel's arm and they walked fast against the wind to make it home.

' It's going to rain at last,' Nili stated. ' You're a farmer, you should know.'

' It might. That was the way my father met my step-mother.'

' In the rain.'

' No. She told him he could stay the night, and he did.'

' Well, don't worry.' They were climbing the stairs to the flat now. ' I'm not about to marry you, or anybody. So you have a father? '

She gave him the key, rubbing her chilled arms, and he opened the door and fumbled for the light.

' Yes, I have a father, he lives in Beer-Sheba. Don't you? '

' And a mother, and a younger sister, and a brother in the army. Do you like jazz? '

' Sort of. I'd better go to sleep or I won't be able to make it for work in the morning.'

' O.K.' she said. ' Don't mind me. I never go to sleep before two. When you leave in the morning you can take this key. I have a spare one.'

' I'll look for a room tomorrow.'

' No hurry.'

She moved the record-player to the kitchen and he was

lying in bed in the dark listening to the music when it started to rain.

*   *   *

The doctor injected Kalinsky to ease his pain.
' You'll fall asleep soon,' he said.
' What's the use? ' Kalinsky murmured.
The light was off in the room and the white partition closed in on him. He was thinking of Mina, the boys' mother. He wondered why he thought of her so seldom, and why should he think of her now? Young laughter reached him from the street and he could see chestnuts when he closed his eyes. Tall green chestnut trees along the river. And the slope, the wild park, a meeting-place for lovers, Okromglaak, where he proposed to Mina. He couldn't remember exactly what words he used or what she said. He remembered they decided to wait until he finished his studies, and he remembered he thought he was lucky. Mina was a beautiful girl, and perhaps it had never occurred to him that she might refuse him. Large green chestnut trees, he could see them now. He was going to be buried in Gilad, in the green forest, there were no chestnut trees there, but still, it was better than this treeless landscape he lived in. Where do lovers go in Beer-Sheba, he wondered. No river, no forest, and the dunes hugging the city offered mystery, but no hiding-places.
Mina was a virgin. He had kissed her once or twice and held her body but she was a virgin when they married. He was a virgin too. Little Shmuel is happy, he thought, so maybe it was all worthwhile. He has never seen chestnut trees, never seen a river. But he will walk one day with a girl, to the dunes or the wadi – he heard laughter again –

the way his mother did. The pain melted away, and his hands felt heavy, footsteps echoed occasionally in his mind, running, pacing, walking down slopes to the river, steady, floating, barely touching the ground.

Daniel was measuring the road. Very slowly, first along the asphalt, then along the unpaved hard surface which became softer and softer and when he stopped he was on top of a hill overlooking the city. He should visit Nechama, he thought. Would she let him in without uniform, not wearing the red beret? Nechama was an immense night, protective and tranquil. He could close his eyes with her and disappear, she was never really with him, it could have been someone else and yet he was there, with her, inside her, beside her. Nili was sunshine, night and day, a bright warm intangible beam. He could hear jazz, then the raindrops tapping on the shutters, then her body next to his, the first night.

* * *

' The first rain,' she said, and came to lie next to him. ' I'm cold.' She lifted the thin cover and slipped in. ' Were you asleep? '

' Hush,' he said. ' You talk too much.'

She continued to talk. Her hands were along his body and she was no different in bed than in the kitchen, or in the café, or in the street.

' Do you like to make love? Don't think I ask strangers in every night, and jump into their bed. Do you think I do? I like you. Perhaps I will like you more and more, maybe less and less, but can you hear the rain? Please talk to me.'

' What can I say? You're lovely. I don't know what

I'm doing here, and tomorrow, I have to think about tomorrow. Well it isn't here yet, it's now.'

And Nili was always now and he was making love to her on the small unstable bed and she was talking.

' We're so silly, ' she said, her hands deep in his hair. ' The other bed is more comfortable, shall we move? '

' Please don't talk.'

She giggled.

Nili's giggle, coloured candy, raindrops on tin, coins in a can. Nili's body. He was sitting on the ground smoothing the sand now. Among the lights below, he could discern the hospital's. He was very tired. As if he had always been seventeen, and then suddenly he was twenty-seven and the leap was too demanding. His father was dying, he knew, and his sister was pregnant and Nili was asleep somewhere, right now, in the arms of someone, dreaming up new names for bottles and new shapes for shoes. Even Nili slept sometimes.

He left her asleep on the small bed in the morning to go to the bus station. Her fair hair drew a pattern on the pillow and her hands rested near a hot neck, folded and young. He felt light and oddly happy and only for a brief moment the image of yesterday's mongoloid child crept into his mind to be driven away by that of Nili saying: ' We should celebrate.' He was used to hard work and there was something relaxing about the roar of the engine, the heavy movement of the bulldozer, the upturned and lifted earth and the sight of other men, muscled and perspiring, naked to the waist. He forgot to buy food and one of the men offered him his.

In the afternoon he returned to the city, to Nili's city, Nili's street, Nili's house. The flat was empty. She had made the bed and brought more flowers in and near the

168

flower-vase a note scribbled in a childish handwriting in green pencil and the largest possible script. ' Nili will not be late,' it read, ' don't dream of leaving. Does anyone ever call you Danny?'

He made some tea and fell asleep to wake up in darkness, not knowing what the time was and Nili still gone. There was some food in the kitchen and he ate, wrote a letter to Rina, looked through the records and the books (Sartre, Camus, Wilde, a book on dancing, an Anthology of English Poetry) and sat down to look through the window. A street full of windows, and lights in the windows, and the faces of people and backs of people and women carrying food to tables and a woman with a child and a young man looking out and talking to someone in the street. And more windows down the street which he could not see clearly but could imagine the people behind them, and there was something unbearable about it. They were not him. They had never seen Daniel Kalinsky and had never heard of him, never heard of Nili – who filled the universe. They all had hands and heads and plans and dreams and little wallets with pictures of more people, and other people walked in the street. They were wearing clothes which they bought in shops, chose, rejecting others, tried on, had fitted. They had thoughts and they were not him, he had never met them, they had never seen him, they didn't care. And if there were other windows, perhaps there were other cities, other countries, other worlds, more stars and billions of people having dinner, laughing, making love, liking garlic or disliking lamb. They all had legs, and tongues and hair and teeth and he laughed at himself thinking about it and felt sick. They talked, they answered questions, he did not know them, he would never know them, how could he, they

169

were not Daniel, they had other names, other faces, other desires. He closed the shutters in anger, anger and unfathomable sadness. Just then the door was flung open and Nili walked in. ' Guess who's here!' she said and put her arms around his neck stepping out of her shoes at the same time.

' You look so worried,' she said.

' What's the time?'

' You're a grown-up boy, you should have a watch. It's almost midnight, did you eat? Had a good day?'

While she was talking, never saying anything about where she had been, she undressed and he had never seen anybody undress fast as Nili. Here she was a bundle of colours and stockings and her hair tied back in a ribbon looking like a little girl and less than a moment later, a naked woman in the bed, eager and inviting.

' Let's make love,' she said and impatiently watched him wash and undress. ' Let's do it with the lights on, so you can see me,' she added, ' and I'll let you sleep afterwards.'

And there was Beer-Sheba, a Nili-less city. More windows, more doors, more unknown people, except that he had learned not to care any more. He had stopped seeing them, lost them all one day, and he now cared for himself even less. He could place himself in one of those square lit openings and watch it and say ' there are all these creatures, and there is one Daniel Kalinsky, another grain in the unfamiliar desert, and he has legs and hands and a mind and a beginning and an end and a lifespan in between and he will leave no mark upon this earth. Will his father? Another window in the distance, with a cough and a pain and an odour and a leftover of a body. He leaves children behind, as insignificant as he is,

170

memories in people's minds which will perish and disappear sooner or later.' He touched the soft sand, Nili's belly, her breasts, her thighs. She used to tease him and call him Danny which he disliked. She used to laugh at his clothes, and made him buy a suit. She said she would knit for him and never did, she tried to cook, she danced and laughed and never said I love you. Neither did he. She never asked questions and often called him ' stranger,' which he was, and chose to remain. He didn't see Rina, and he didn't see his father. He built a road during the day and Nili filled his nights. They seldom went out together and when she was out and back late she never failed to wake him up saying – ' Wake up, stranger, Nili is here,' or – ' who's sleeping in my bed,' or – ' I must tell you something.' One week-end he went to Gilad and he returned that same night. She simply said – ' I knew you'd miss me ' and cuddled in his arms, gratitude in her big eyes.

A month went by and he was handed a cheque which almost covered the tickets for Haim and Dora. They were to go by boat to Trieste and then by train to Warsaw. Two more weeks and it would all be over. But he refused to think about leaving Nili. He didn't have to think about it, things simply happened.

One evening he returned from work and found her in bed. Nili, who believed that all diseases were psychological, was in bed, ill, pale, her stare hard and detached.

' News for you stranger.' She was not smiling. ' I've been to a doctor. It was awful.'

' What happened?'

' Everything. I found out a week ago I was pregnant and today I had an abortion and it's all over and not to worry and I have to stay in bed a day or two.' He thought she was joking, then he thought she was lying, though he knew it was the truth and he lost control.

' It was nothing,' she said.

' Just why didn't you tell me? Before? It was my child too wasn't it? Or am I just someone to hold at night, a comfortable body?'

' Don't be dramatic. You're so banal. I didn't want to trouble you, what's the use? The result would have been the same.'

' What makes you so sure?'

' I didn't want your child.'

' What did you want? What do you want?'

' Come on stranger, we had a good time, we were free, I knew you'd leave soon, you have to, so it was perfect, and then this happened and now it's over. I could have hidden it from you, you know, say I had the flu or something.'

' Well thanks for being truthful.'

He walked out into the street and around the block and when he returned the light was off and he tiptoed to his camp bed and undressed in the dark.

' I'm not asleep,' she said.

She was crying. He sat on her bed and watched her cry until dawn. There was nothing to say and her tears had the quality of her laughter, flowing and friendly and engulfing and she did not ask forgiveness, those were her private tears, Nili's tears, and he was unable to pardon. In the morning he went to his boss, received some money and bought two tickets to Warsaw. In the flat he found a note, ' Nili is gone,' and he started packing.

Chapter Ten

His fingers sifted the sand gently and he watched it form a heap in front of him, golden purity. He destroyed it and started walking towards town. He was going to visit Nechama. Nili happened so fast, one day she was all there and the next day she was gone and he never thought of looking for her. She didn't want his child. She didn't ask him whether he wanted it, she didn't want him either, and this didn't disturb him. He was going to look for Nechama and Kalinsky summoned the nurse for another injection.

How lost the city looked at night, small, empty, helpless. He walked to his house and noticed that he had left the light on. I could go in now he thought. To the second floor, to his room and his bed, and wake him up. I could hold his hand and watch him die. Watch my father die. I could talk to him, say good things, tell happy tales, tell him the night is good. He walked on through the central bus station, along the main street to Nechama's house. Orion was high above him, it must be long past midnight he thought, climbing the stairs to the familiar door.

' Who is it?' she said.

' Daniel. Are you alone?'

She opened the door, a changed unsmiling woman. ' Am I alone,' she said, ' yes, I am alone. You forget an element called time. Come in.'

Time had not affected the flat, its smell or its atmosphere. Had she turned the lights off the years would have crawled back to the white breasts and the round body and the black hair on the white pillow, to Yoram, to years without Kalinsky, without Nili. It was not with a sudden shock that he noticed the change in her, but with a slow lingering realization. Her black hair was dyed now and there was something artificial about it. She made coffee and when she bent down to put his cup on the low table, he noticed her breast, Nechama's full breasts, and he thought of his father shrinking behind the white partition. There was something forced in her laughter, and the smoothness of her arms was gone. She lit a cigarette and the flame threw a shadow under her eyes, her fallen cheeks. Nechama's flabby arms, thin ankles, swollen feet. ' It happened fast,' she said. ' The boys stopped coming.'

' It's a different generation,' he suggested.

' It's the age,' she murmured.

' You look well,' he lied.

' A lonely woman never looks well. I'll tell you what happened the other day, at Morris's.' He was listening. ' I had dinner alone, in a corner and some paratroopers were talking around a table next to mine. They talked about a legendary woman. They had just arrived in Beer-Sheba and they had nothing to do. " It used to be different," they said. " The unit had a woman once, not a whore, a woman. She lived here and she was beautiful and they were her lovers, her sons, her friends. She loved them all and they loved her and she was their good luck charm. She knew the ones who died, they left for battle with her memory and she was something to come back to." Another sighed and said, " why don't we find

174

one too," and then the sergeant among them said, " you don't find women like that, they find you, they just happen to you." Then one of them asked, " what do you think happened to her," and the first one said, " she must be an old hag by now and a woman knows when the game ends." They left to see a movie and they never so much as looked at me.' She had a wise smile on her face. There was no sadness in her eyes and he had nothing to say. ' I happened to them, to you, to your friend Yoram, to all of you. Perhaps I only happened to the first one, the one I loved. You're not married are you?'

He laughed. ' Not at all, no plans either.'

' What are you doing here?'

' Come to visit my father, he's in hospital dying.'

' Well, it's a hospital you know well. Are you staying long?'

' A few days, depending.'

' Still in Gilad?'

' On and off.'

And there was nothing else to say. Little bridges above time, across a wrinkled face. How are you, what do you do, where do you live, how is the family? Bridges hanging above precipitous gaps trying to touch the other side, nostalgically – do you remember? What happened to him? Do you recall . . . And the ironic grin of memory trying to erase the wrinkles grows more distinct and subtly reality takes over and there is Nechama – an old worn-out woman. It couldn't go on any more. One day the last one came. He was new and fresh and I was his first woman and all of a sudden I saw there was a little boy in my bed whose skin was fresher than mine and I burst out laughing. He never returned and the others drifted away. At times they visit, like you tonight. He shook her hand to bid her

175

farewell and she embraced him. He held her for a moment and left quietly. ' I'll come again,' he said. She opened the window and watched him walk up the street, a grown-up man, joyless and measured.

For the first time in many years he resented being alone. He fell asleep with dawn, leaving the lights on and the windows open.

In the morning he decided to go and visit Rina. He had nothing to do and the flat was empty. He told Lipsky he was going away. Lipsky never asked him anything.

' If Miriam asks tell her I'll be back soon.'

And he walked to the crossroad at the southern entrance to the city, to the bridge. A hot day and no cars on the road. An army lorry approached. He shyly waved his hand trying to hail it. The car didn't stop. The advantage of uniform on the road, he thought just as a civilian jeep stopped near him. ' Want a lift?' the driver asked. ' Yes please.' He climbed in. The driver was a middle-aged man, gray-haired and tanned. You could tell a desert dweller by the look of his skin. He knew the road well and avoided the lumps – the best car in the world he said. Daniel agreed.

' Ever driven one?'

' In the army.' He mentioned his unit which produced a look of respect on the man's face.

' Where would you like to go?'

' Where are you going?'

' To the Phosphate Plant. I've been going there for years, since it started.'

' I'll get off at the corner and wait for another lift.'

The road folded under the wheels like a metal ribbon and the roar of the engine inhibited conversation. Daniel felt the warm familiar wind blowing at his face and he wished the journey would never end when the jeep came to a halt. He jumped off and started walking downhill. First walking, then taking off his sandals and running along the soft shoulders of the asphalt road until he was breathless.

The sun had reached its zenith and he was thirsty. A few Bedouins were gathered round a well in the distance and he walked towards them for some water.

Kalinsky's lips were dry. His mouth was dry, so was his throat all the way down to his lungs and the pain subsided when he drank, only to return more strongly later. It was a bearable pain, but it promised a worse one and he knew he was at the end. No thoughts of another world, paradise or hell, no thoughts altogether. He lived with the apathy of the dying, succumbing to it willingly, emerging from it and reaching for the bell and again sinking with it and drifting away. He was careful not to touch his body as the touch irritated him and he avoided looking at his arms stretched in front of him above the sheet. He fixed his stare at the ceiling, the ventilator and at times the window and when a thought came into his mind he felt too weak to grasp it.

The doctor said they would move him to a private room and the doctor's voice reached him through many layers of soft cottonwool, echoless and numbing. A long trip followed. They removed the partition and lowered his bed and Rachel came in to roll him out. He didn't open his eyes but sensed the low movement. It didn't feel like a horizontal trip along corridors, but a downhill one and he wondered whether he was in some secret passage which bypassed the stairs leading to the ground floor. Closer to the morgue. When they stopped he thought he was still moving and the pain was renewed. He opened his eyes. The room was different. For a second he thought he was at home, in Warsaw, his parents' home and he could hear them talking in the living room. ' Your son is very sick.' his mother told his father. ' He will recover, he is a healthy boy and the doctor the best there is.'

He knew he was in Warsaw, because of the smell in the room and the snowflakes against the window. ' What is it? ' he heard a strange voice ask. He must have been talking aloud because a blurred image of Rachel confronted him, very closely, very dark against the white curtain. There was a small spare bed in the new room and his personal belongings were placed in a new cupboard. The smell of disinfectant overpowered the Warsaw odour and he closed his eyes again. He was waiting.

*   *   *

Daniel had some water from the well and chatted with the Bedouins. They knew a short cut to the excavations and offered to take him there. After a few minutes he changed his mind. ' I have to go back to Beer-Sheba,' he said, ' how do I get to the main road? ' They didn't seem to understand but accepted it when he turned in the opposite direction and started walking fast, almost running. The road, straight as a ruler and carless, met his eye. Getting back was a question of luck. Two over-crowded cars swept by, a motorcycle – a girl glued to the rider's back – and then silence again, disturbed only by a southerly wind carrying sand and sprinkling it along the road like grains of salt. He didn't want to see Rina. He knew she would preach and ask and scold and he wasn't up to it. He didn't want to be alone either, because his aloneness like never before was invaded by ghostly memories and he knew he should visit his father or it would be too late.

Not that it mattered. The old man would die anyway and Daniel didn't believe it mattered how you died or what you carried with you to the grave. But what you left behind did matter. Daniel was one of the things Haim would leave behind, and somehow visiting or not visiting his father had to do with his value as a legacy. There were no cars in sight and, exasperated, he measured with his steps the road towards the city, turning his head back every now and again hoping to see a car emerging from behind the low hills.

*   *   *

When Kalinsky regained consciousness he heard Dora's voice. She was lying on the spare bed in his room and he thought they were at home. He asked her about the shop's turnover that day and then, ' Why do you cry Dora? ' and she mumbled something which escaped him. ' Did Miriam come by? ' he asked, and she managed to answer casually. ' Shall I get you some water Dora? ' and then, ' How many years have we been married? ' and, ' I feel a pain in the chest.' He saw that Dora was wearing a dress. ' Why are you dressed up Dora? Where are we? '

*   *   *

Two cars passed Daniel going in the opposite direction. Both drivers stopped and asked if he needed anything and he continued to walk. With nightfall a heavy lorry stopped for him and it felt like the end of a battle. The lights in the wilderness, the minaret, the bridge. He went to eat at Morris's and decided to go and see Miriam after dinner. Perhaps they could go and visit Haim together. He felt like seeing little Shmuel. Miriam opened the door. She was not surprised to see him.

' Did you get my message? ' she asked.

' No, I was out of town, just came back. How is he? '

' Come in. Shmuel asked about you.'

They entered the room and he wondered whether Kalinsky was dead and Miriam was slowly breaking the news to him. He thought of Nili not asking him about the baby and stopped cold.

' I asked you how my father was.'

' He just is. He had a haemorrhage.'

' When was that? '

' In the afternoon. Mother is with him. He's unconscious now. Perhaps it's a matter of hours, or a day, I don't know. I wasn't feeling well and didn't stay and talk to the doctor. Did you have dinner? '

Her husband entered the room holding Shmuel in his arms. He lowered the boy who ran towards Daniel and pointed a toy gun at him laughing.

' Will you stay? Can we play a new game? '

' I'll play a game if you like.'

' Leave Uncle Daniel alone now,' Miriam said and went out into the kitchen. He had never been alone with Miriam's husband and what could he say to him? Tell him about the baby, about Nechama? Talk to him about his shop, business, the banana plantation at Gilad?

' Have you seen my father? ' he asked.

' No, you know how it is, one of us has to stay with the boy and tend the shop now that Dora is with him.'

'Do you like Beer-Sheba?' He regretted the question once asked, but the answer was straight 'Of course. Why else would I be here? It's different, and special, and Miriam likes it.'

'My father doesn't.'

'Doesn't he? He would have hated Tel-Aviv. Beer-Sheba bothers him physically that's all.'

'Not that it makes a difference now.'

'Well, I have heard of miracles, last minute recoveries, you never know.'

Daniel knew very well, and so did Miriam, and when their looks met it seemed that they communicated this knowledge and he was grateful to her. He liked having a sister that evening and the boy took him to his bedroom for a bedtime story.

Surprisingly enough, Daniel accepted Miriam's husband's invitation to play a game of chess. Shmuel was in bed and some records were put on and Daniel felt he had been there many times before, and that they were his family. Miriam was mending a dress, sitting upright on her chair. Her big pregnant belly looked firm and round and somehow she projected tranquillity. He lost the game without caring much.

'You play well,' his partner apologized for winning, 'I imagine you didn't concentrate. You know I lost my father last year.' Daniel didn't know. At times he even forgot his name. He got up and put his hand on Miriam's neck.

'You must be tired, why don't you go to sleep?'

'I have to leave too.' Daniel got up.

Was it pity in Miriam's eyes when she said goodnight to him?

'When are you expecting?' he asked when leaving.

' Next month.'

' If you'd like to, you can send Shmuel to Gilad for a week or two. It will make it easier for you and I'd enjoy it.'

' Thank you.' A trace of a smile, her husband's large comforting hand and he was alone again.

*　　*　　*

Kalinsky was with Dora but he was not aware of it. The man said there were miraculous recoveries sometimes, but it didn't look as if Haim was going to be the object of a miracle. Dora watched him shamelessly. She never did before. She had never looked at him in a detailed thorough way, she had never seen him helpless, not even at the beginning when she offered him shelter. She was already thinking about life without Haim, and it was going to be a long pull without him. She was younger, she was healthy and she had a daughter, a grandchild, a shop, a way of life. She watched her husband closely. The contours of his face were sharper than ever but the skin was not badly wrinkled. The hands were long and delicate and she held them in her own. He was a useless, helpless child, a dying bird and she accepted it. She accepted it with all the desperate agony acceptance can hold. She didn't believe in miracles, but she wanted to talk to him. She wanted to thank him for bringing her there. She walked to the window and let the cool air in. It was her city putting out its lights ready for a short night's sleep. She liked talking to Mrs Lipsky and when she did she was ashamed of the things they said. They were bitter, nostalgic, irritated, but this was all part of the life in her city. She had the privilege of complaining, of choosing, of disagreeing and disliking.

182

The doctor came in and examined Haim. ' I am afraid there isn't much I can do. You ought to get some sleep too. I'll have the nurse look in from time to time.'

' Will he have much pain? '

' As long as he is unconscious he is free of it. We'll see tomorrow. Do your children know? '

' Our daughter was here today. His son knows.'

' There is some tea in the doctor's room on this floor, help yourself whenever you feel like it.'

' Good night doctor.'

She took a walk along the corridor. She was curious about the other patients. Were their wives in tears? She felt guilty about her curiosity but paused to listen to sighs of pain, to two patients whispering to each other. Through the night from the Maternity Ward flashed the scream of a woman, once only. She returned to her husband but he hadn't moved. The nurse left some food for her which she didn't touch. She sat on the white chair, the way she used to in the other room during visiting hours, and fell asleep. The spare bed remained empty and the night nurse who looked in once thought she was wrapped in thoughts and sadness.

Sadness was what Daniel felt walking home. When Yoram died it was a passionate anger, it was revolt, it was a world shaken and crumbling pillars. When he lost Nili, when Nili gave up his baby, it was self-pity and hurt vanity. And now sadness entered the corridors of his being, ignoring the open doors to rooms cluttered with unhappy memories and settling in. Sadness evaporating and clinging to ceiling and corners, sadness which plasters the walls

183

and becomes a second nature. He hurried up and opened the window. He was not told about the new room and there was no light in the second-floor windows. He presumed Dora was asleep too and there was nothing to do but wait until the morning. He was alone in the world, with Kalinsky. He was seeing him clearly, now, as clear as on their last meeting, then too they were alone. ' Nili is gone ' the note said and he packed and left. The bus to Beer-Sheba left five minutes before he reached the station and he took a taxi. He went straight to the shop and his father was there completing the accounts of the day, preparing to go home. Dora came in and greeted him and Haim merely said, ' You don't visit us very often.'

' I want to talk to you,' Daniel said. ' I have to go back tonight.'

' We'll go to the house.'

The night was cold and heavy with clouds. The clay road was muddy because it had rained in the morning and the misery of a winter night never became Beer-Sheba. Clad in coats and walking far apart from each other, an outsider would never have identified them as a family returning home.

The roof leaked that winter and two bowls were placed in the middle of the room to catch the raindrops. It was cold in the house and they sat in the kitchen which smelt of fumes from the kerosene stove.

' How are you doing these days? '

' Why should I burden you? ' Haim said, ' We manage. It's not what we expected to find, but we have enough to eat and clothes to wear. The rest is troubles.' Daniel listened carefully for a while, and his father listed his complaints. The plumber was charging too much, people asked for credit in the shop and never paid, they were never prepared for the winter. Miriam had stopped coming every day since the child was born and the mayor was prejudiced against the Poles. Dora excused herself and he heard her wash and undress. He heard her enter the bed, he heard the bedsprings move under her weight and he heard her twist and turn. How could he talk to his father? He took an envelope out of his coat pocket. ' I have been doing a lot of thinking.' He was at a loss now. ' It doesn't work for you, so, I brought you something.'

Kalinsky first looked at his son, heavily resigned to not understanding him fully long ago, then took the envelope and opened it. ' A gift? ' he said, smiling before he saw the tickets. He stood up pale and suddenly tall. ' What are these? '

Daniel looked up. There was something impudent in his glance.

' It hasn't worked out for you here, and I feel responsible. You shouldn't be prevented from going back, that is if you want to.' The man in front of him opened his mouth as if to say something, and then he slapped him. His cheek burned and his first reaction was to hit back, when he remembered it was his father. He never knew what gave Haim the strength and courage to hit him that night.

' I didn't mean it. That way. I thought you were unhappy here.' He talked fast now, trying to explain himself, inventing excuses.

' Look at the way you live,' he said. ' With the rain in winter and the heat in the summer, with that little shop which demands all your time and doesn't supply half your needs. You hate the place, you hate the people, you hate the mayor and the streets and even the stones and the hills. You came to see me, now we've met and you can go back.'

His father was grinning. He was holding the envelope and he handed it back to Daniel.

' I have nothing to say to you. You can take this gift and walk out of here, and you don't need to return. You don't understand anything – you are spoiled and protected and your mind isn't capable of existing even in the small circle you exist in. So the roof is leaking? Do you expect me not to complain? Of course the plumber overcharges, and I can't afford to do half the things I would have liked to do but what is the answer? So take this answer you have produced and go away, and live some more and when you are ready to apologize come back. I won't tell Dora anything, or Miriam, I am ashamed to. Good night.'

' But, father . . . ' and the door was shut behind him.

He let the rain wash his face. Nili has gone he thought and he had two tickets to Warsaw in his pocket. Perhaps if he had the right to reject his own father, Nili had the right to reject his child. The rain formed puddles and he walked around them. He walked to Rina's flat. Lipsky downstairs had the key. He would never return to his father's house he decided. Rina was away and the flat needed a fresh whitewash. He looked at the hospital then, little suspecting that a long time later he would be standing at the same window staring at a blind window behind which his father lay dying.

*   *   *

It was summer and no chance of rain but he thought he heard raindrops and the sound of Nili crying. ' When you slapped my face Kalinsky, once again you were not a common man and once again I couldn't forgive you.'

186

Behind the window across the road another patient occupied a white iron bed and in a small private room Kalinsky was lying still.

But not dead yet. He didn't know the difference between night and day but his weak pulse indicated life. The sun was up and for once it did not bother him, but his consumed body still had life in it and Dora sat on the white chair waiting for a sign, a sign of life or of death, a movement to redeem her from this long wait. Daniel washed and shaved, put on a clean shirt. He brewed some Lipsky coffee and tidied the place up. The street was being swept and Lipsky unlocked the glass doors and placed the tables and chairs on the terrace. Daniel crossed the street to the entrance gate and walked through the hall to the second floor. A strange bold man occupied his father's bed and as he grabbed the arm of the first doctor he saw:

' Where is Kalinsky? '

' Who is Kalinsky? '

' My father.'

' You'd better ask downstairs, it's not my ward.'

He returned to the lobby and the information desk. A crippled man was sitting behind the desk. ' Can I help you? ' he asked.

' I hope so . . . Kalinsky, Haim. He was on the second floor until yesterday.' The man had one hand only and with maddening slowness managed to reach for the right list to look for the name.

' I have it,' he said triumphantly. He was new in the hospital, a social case. ' The first floor, a private room. Any of the nurses on the floor will direct you.'

Daniel knew what a private room meant, he had been through it before, and the memory of Yoram's parents crossed his mind. A nurse directed him to a closed door

187

and he hesitated in front of it. He knocked and Dora's voice answered, ' Come in.' All he could see at first was the crumpled white sheets and Dora's heavy body on the small chair. The bed looked empty but as he approached he realized that what he thought were merely creases in the bed linen were his father's thin limbs. Ignoring Dora he grasped his father's arm and felt for the pulse. ' Not yet,' Dora whispered.

' Will he regain consciousness? '

' The doctor doubts it.'

' I have to talk to him,' he said. Dora didn't ask him why he had waited so long. She didn't give him a reproaching look, she didn't give him any particular look. He stood between her and Haim, but there was nothing between her and her husband, nothing but the smell of drugs and thin sheets.

' I saw Miriam last night. She told me about the haemorrhage.'

' It doesn't matter now. He feels no pain.'

Daniel couldn't accept, the way healthy people cannot, complete unconsciousness. He wished Dora wasn't there. He was sure he could hold his father and gently wake him up and talk to him, whisper to him and perhaps hear him say something, anything.

The doctor came in an hour later. He held his hand, felt for the pulse and laid the arm on the bed back in place.

' His suffering is over,' he said. ' He is dead. I'm sorry.'

Simply so. One shameless word and it was all over. He looked at the corpse on the bed and shivered. ' My father is dead,' he said. ' He's not suffering any more.'

A hand touched his shoulder and the image on the bed changed its face. It was Yoram asleep and the hand was Rina's and he touched it to feel a softness Rina never had.

Miriam's cheeks were wet and she hurt his arm now. He
took her in his arms. Their father was dead. Dora was
sobbing on the spare bed and the doctor gave her an
injection.

' You're crying,' Miriam told Daniel.

' I wanted to tell him something.'

Briefly the grief separated itself from the dead. The
three people were involved with their sorrow and the
relaxed muscles of Kalinsky's face gave it a smooth
appearance. A nurse came in, suggested Miriam leave,
and Dora was taken to another room. Daniel was left
alone with his father.

*   *   *

He waited until they rolled the bed away and walked into
the street. Lipsky was wiping his hands on his white
apron and Mrs Lipsky quarrelling with a Bedouin family
who had camped on the stairs leading to the terrace. A
car sounded its horn in spite of the sign ' Silence –
Hospital ', and the sun melted an ice block left in front
of one of the houses. Daniel looked at the faces of the
people and some turned to look back at him because he
was walking fast and staring at them fixedly. A woman's
laughter could be heard from a second floor and the
pedlar was shouting,' Anything for twenty piastres '. He
had balloons and plastic toys, cheap cups and wooden
dolls. Daniel reached the main street and slowed his pace.
They didn't know. A man spat from an open car window
and a woman said, ' Disgusting.' A group of school-
children crossed the street in pairs holding up the traffic.

The waiter at ' Eshel ' waved to Daniel and Daniel
waved back. It wasn't his fault, he didn't know either.

189

What will they tell Shmuel, he wondered. Will they tell him his grandfather went to heaven? On a trip? Disappeared? God took him? What do they tell little children now? A command car stopped in front of a kiosk for evening papers and the market was crowded and alive. Somewhere in the morgue on the stretcher they were washing up his father, but the street was ignorant. He didn't mind. He didn't want to stop them and tell them, he didn't care to share it with them, he wasn't disturbed any more by not knowing who died for them that day. He had a secret and that made him different. His cheeks were wet and they were laughing and that made him special. His father died that morning and they were bargaining about cheaper grapes and that made it all move forward.

He returned to the hospital. Miriam was downstairs waiting for Dora and they were given a parcel from the nurse. Kalinsky's belongings.

' Would you like to keep anything? ' his sister asked.

' The watch, if I may.' He was given the large old-fashioned watch, and he put it on.

' He wanted to be buried in Gilad,' Miriam said. ' Do you think it can be done? '

' Yes. I'd better leave today and make the arrangements. I don't think you'll need my help here.'

The green took over. He was going north again. His father wanted to be buried in black earth, near water and trees and his son.

He returned to his room as if from a battle and people came in to shake his hand and murmur a few words of condolence. He arranged for the funeral with the Kibbutz secretary. He fell asleep in the afternoon and woke up the following morning.

*　　*　　*

190

Cemetery Hill. Walks with Rina to look for plants and later for sherds. Walks with Yoram to drink in the view. Climbing alone with a book on a free day, burying Yoram, visiting the grave. Gilad's earth is kind to the dead, warm and protective, and the new grave looked more natural than the last one he had seen. The family arrived and the black car carried Kalinsky up the hill. Miriam made it with difficulty, supported by her husband, and Daniel asked Kibbutz members not to participate.

He had learned the words of the Kaddish and his trembling voice sounded the prayer. ' Do you ever pray? ' the rabbi in Jerusalem asked him. He was praying now as they lowered his father's body and covered it with earth. ' Yitgadal veyitkadash shmei Raba . . . ' words strange to him echoed and rolled down the hill past Yoram's tomb, flowed south with the Jordan and filled the valley.

About the Author

YAËL DAYAN was born in 1939 in Nahalal, a village near Nazareth in Israel. She studied at the Hebrew University of Jerusalem, and later entered the Israeli army in 1956, serving as a Lieutenant for two years. During this period she wrote her first novel, *New Face in the Mirror,* which was widely acclaimed. In the years that followed, Miss Dayan wrote two more novels, *Envy the Frightened* and *Dust,* a travel book, and numerous articles in the Hebrew and foreign press. She has travelled in Europe, South America, Africa and the Far East, lectures every year in America, and spends part of her time in Greece, where this novel was written.

The daughter of Israel's General Moshe Dayan, Yaël Dayan is single, has two brothers, speaks Hebrew, English, Greek and French, and writes her novels in English.